1-8.17. — 1-9-17.

Please return on or before the latest date above.
You can renew online at *www.kent.gov.uk/libs*
or by telephone 08458 247 200

_____

_____

Libraries & Archives

00884\DTP\RN\07.07   LIB 7

SPECIAL MESSAGE TO READERS

THE ULVERSCROFT FOUNDATION
(registered UK charity number 264873)
was established in 1972 to provide funds for
research, diagnosis and treatment of eye diseases.
Examples of major projects funded by
the Ulverscroft Foundation are:-

- The Children's Eye Unit at Moorfields Eye Hospital, London
- The Ulverscroft Children's Eye Unit at Great Ormond Street Hospital for Sick Children
- Funding research into eye diseases and treatment at the Department of Ophthalmology, University of Leicester
- The Ulverscroft Vision Research Group, Institute of Child Health
- Twin operating theatres at the Western Ophthalmic Hospital, London
- The Chair of Ophthalmology at the Royal Australian College of Ophthalmologists

You can help further the work of the Foundation
by making a donation or leaving a legacy.
Every contribution is gratefully received. If you
would like to help support the Foundation or
require further information, please contact:

THE ULVERSCROFT FOUNDATION
The Green, Bradgate Road, Anstey
Leicester LE7 7FU, England
Tel: (0116) 236 4325

website: www.foundation.ulverscroft.com

LAST DAY IN PARADISE

When professional gambler Jimmy 'the Kid' Casey beats the son of wealthy ranch owner Jack Hartigan in a game of poker, he is forced to shoot the young man dead in self-defence. Hartigan vows revenge and the card player flees the town of Paradise, only to find himself pursued by a gang of killers led by Abe Morgan. Things become more complicated when the gang captures Jimmy's fiancée, and renegade Apaches go on the warpath . . .

Books by Paul Green
in the Linford Western Library:

THE DEVIL'S PAYROLL

PAUL GREEN

◆

LAST DAY IN PARADISE

Complete and Unabridged

LINFORD
Leicester

First published in Great Britain in 2013 by
Robert Hale Limited
London

First Linford Edition
published 2015
by arrangement with
Robert Hale Limited
London

A catalogue record for this book is available
from the British Library.

ISBN 978–1–4448–2247–2

Published by
F. A. Thorpe (Publishing)
Anstey, Leicestershire

Set by Words & Graphics Ltd.
Anstey, Leicestershire
Printed and bound in Great Britain by
T. J. International Ltd., Padstow, Cornwall

This book is printed on acid-free paper

*To the real Jimmy 'the Kid' Casey,
the most famous man in Cork*

1

Jimmy Casey drew in the reins of his palomino as he approached the weather-beaten sign bearing the words *Welcome to Paradise*. The town was set in an area of grassland watered by a spring and there were cattle grazing in the fields beyond. To a man who had just spent several days riding through the Chiricahua desert in the Arizona basin, the sight seemed like paradise indeed. Another long stretch of desert lay ahead and there were no other towns between here and the trading post at Fort Bowie so he decided to rest up for a day or two before continuing his journey.

The town looked peaceful at first sight, its dusty main street lined with clapboard and adobe buildings. He passed a grocery and hardware store, a gunsmith's and the jail before reaching a livery which advertised stabling, feed and grooming for a dollar a day. Jimmy dismounted before handing the reins to the owner, a grizzled old timer who puffed away on a horn-rimmed pipe.

'I may decide to stay an extra day. Will that be all right?'

'Sure, got plenty of room, mister, though why anyone would want to stay longer than a day in this place beats me.'

'I could do with the rest and so could my horse. The desert starts to get mighty hot at this time of year.'

'It sure does,' replied the livery owner as he caught the silver dollar Jimmy tossed him. 'There's a hotel with a saloon just up the street. It's the only place to stay but it's clean and comfortable.'

'Thanks. Can a man find a good card game around here?'

The old man took in the dark suit and fancy vest of his questioner, the nickel-plated pistols with ivory stocks and the silver band he wore tied around his hat.

'There's always some folks having a card game in the saloon but there ain't much money in it, at least not for a man who makes a living that way.'

Jimmy smiled. 'I see you've guessed my profession.'

'When a man dresses as fancy as you, I reckon he must be either a gambler or a gunfighter and maybe even both.'

Jimmy chuckled, 'The name's Jimmy Casey. What do I call you?'

The old man removed his pipe. 'Clem Bailey. Say, you wouldn't be that fella they call Jimmy the Kid Casey, would you?'

The younger man groaned. 'At the age of thirty-seven I was hoping I might have outgrown the nickname.'

Clem grinned in response. 'When a young pup of eighteen strolls into a joint in Tucson, starts a poker game and walks out with a thousand dollars in his pocket, word gets around. Most folks in these parts have heard the story and it ain't the sort you tend to forget.'

'I guess not, but keep it under your hat, will you?'

The older man winked as he shoved the pipe back into his mouth. 'Good luck with them cards,' was his parting shot as Jimmy wandered off down the street.

A minute later he strode through the bat doors of the saloon and was pleased to note that the floor was carpeted and there was wallpaper in a bright floral design above the wainscoting. Someone had clearly spent money on the place. Perhaps there were some rich pickings in Paradise after all. In April of 1870, with the so called reconstruction under way and the south-west crawling with carpetbaggers, there were not many places left where money was still to be made.

'What can I get you?' asked the bartender, a sprightly man of about sixty with twin tufts of snow-white hair that shot out from behind his ears.

'I'll have a beer, thanks. It's a nice place you've got here. Do you have a room for one, maybe two nights?'

'I sure do, but it's not my place by the way. It belongs to Jack Hartigan, who also owns the ranch and the land around it just outside town.'

From a table in the corner a young man of about twenty turned around in his chair and interrupted the conversation; 'That'll be *Mr* Hartigan to you, Joe, and don't forget it.'

'Sure, Billy. Mr Hartigan it is,' replied the bartender before informing Jimmy in a low whisper that the young man was Jack's only son and his pride and joy.

Jimmy sauntered over to the table where Billy sat with four older men, a small pile of coins and dollar bills in front of him.

'If that's poker you're playing I wouldn't mind joining in.'

Billy looked up from under a tousled mop of mouse-coloured hair, his grey eyes hard and watchful. 'Sure, mister. Sit down if you've got money to lose. I just won the last round.'

Jimmy dropped into a chair and met the younger man's stare with his own piercing blue gaze. Removing his hat, he ran a hand through a head of wiry, raven-coloured hair.

'So, whose turn is it to deal?' he asked.

'It's mine, but I'll sit this one out,' said a stocky, bearded fellow seated on Billy's left. Then he turned to his companion and added, 'Maybe you should quit too while you're ahead. Lady Luck never stays for long.'

'Aw, stop playing nursemaid, Abe. You're Dad's ramrod on the ranch, not my goddamn mother.'

Abe Morgan shrugged. 'OK, suit yourself.'

Billy passed the deck of cards to the man sitting next to Abe, a thin bespectacled fellow who looked like a bank clerk. He shuffled them carefully, asked his neighbour to cut the pack, then dealt five cards to each player.

Jimmy studied his hand carefully. He had a pair but they were high cards, the

6

ten of spades and the ten of hearts. The remaining three were a mixed bag, the two of clubs, six of diamonds and the wild card itself, the joker. He looked around at the other players, trying to read their expressions. The bank clerk was smiling slightly but then suddenly looked up and tried to appear impassive. He might have three of a kind or even a straight, Jimmy figured. Billy Hartigan adopted a self-satisfied smirk as he leaned back in his chair. It seemed a little false to Jimmy's experienced eye, like a man who was consciously trying to seem pleased with himself. He guessed that the youngster was hoping to bluff his companions into supposing he'd a better hand than the one he possessed.

The two remaining players appeared to be concentrating hard. They were a pair of rough-looking individuals in plaid shirts and chaps. Jimmy guessed that they were probably ranch hands. He saw one of them lick his dry lips as he stared morosely at the cards, probably wishing he held better. It was Billy who forced the bet, tossing a ten dollar bill down on to the table.

'That says I've the best hand,' he announced.

'I'll see you,' murmured the clerk as he added another.

One of the ranch hands folded but the other one matched the bet.

'What about you, mister?' asked Billy, fixing Jimmy with an insolent stare.

'I'll raise you another ten.' Jimmy placed twenty dollars on top of the pile as he met his opponent's gaze. Billy smiled and matched the bet. The clerk followed, but a little hesitantly. The other ranch hand folded.

'Let's see what you've got,' said Jimmy.

Billy shook his head. 'That'll cost you another twenty dollars,' he replied, slamming his money down. Jimmy knew he was bluffing but he had the measure of this kid; a spoiled, rich boy who was using his money to force the others out of the game by making bets he knew they could not afford to lose. He decided to play along by letting him win the round. Billy would get careless as success went to his head and Jimmy would be the winner in the next round, after goading the boy into a bigger bet once the time was right.

He pretended to hesitate and then shook his head. 'I guess I'll have to fold.'

'What about you, Seymour?' Billy asked the bank clerk.

The clerk shrugged and put his cards down. Billy laughed and scooped up the money while Abe murmured that they ought to be going.

'I know you don't have to show us, seeing that we've all folded, but I'm curious to know what hand you were holding,' said Jimmy.

'Sure, mister.' Billy showed his cards which included a pair lower than the one Jimmy had and a poorer hand than the three of a kind held by Seymour, who now swore softly. Jimmy slammed his hand down on the table with feigned exasperation and shook his head several times.

'You were bluffing all along, damn it! I should have guessed, but that smile of yours was pretty convincing. Say, how about giving me a chance to win my money back?'

Abe eyed him suspiciously, but Billy shook off the hand tugging at his sleeve. 'OK, but we won't be playing for dimes and cents.'

'That's fine by me.'

Billy sat down again and Jimmy dealt the cards this time. Seymour decided to try his luck just once more but the others stayed out. Jimmy drew a flush, all five cards were hearts and one was a queen. Not bad at all. He glanced up and saw, in Billy Hartigan's eyes, that flash of optimism which the inexperienced and the naive have not yet learned to hide. The boy swallowed hard, which suggested a good hand, a hand that might be good enough to win with luck on your side but not today. No, Jimmy decided, Billy did not have a better hand than he did. Seymour looked hesitant, uncertain before once again adopting that impassive mask. A real gambler did not need to worry about the overly cautious bank clerk who would probably fold after the first bet anyway.

Once again it was Billy who made the first bet, throwing down twenty dollars.

'I'll double that,' said Jimmy nonchalantly.

Seymour looked at his cards, then at the growing pile of money before folding.

'Well, Billy, it's just you and me now. What's it to be?' The trick was to convey the impression that he thought Billy had a poor hand and was bluffing once more. A man believing such a thing would be willing to bet a lot of money that his own cards were better. Billy, thinking that only he knew he was not bluffing would also assume that Jimmy's hand was poorer than his own and fall into the trap.

'I'll raise you another fifty dollars,' said Billy.

'I'm not falling for that this time,' said Jimmy. He drew a hundred dollars from his billfold. 'There, match that and let's see what you've got.'

Billy hesitated for a moment but he was in deep and bravado forced him to continue. He threw down the money, having now committed all his previous winnings to the pot.

There was a momentary pause, then the younger man laid his cards down face up. There were a three of spades, a five of clubs and the eight of diamonds, but accompanied by a pair of aces.

Jimmy gave a low whistle. 'I thought you were bluffing, kid. I didn't figure on those aces being there. Then as he laid his own cards down he added 'It's lucky for me a flush beats any pair.'

The colour drained from Billy's face as Jimmy scooped the money towards him. Then he slowly rose from his chair, his eyes blazing. 'You goddamn card-sharp!' he cried.

Billy Hartigan's pistol was barely out of his holster when he found himself staring down the barrel of Jimmy's nickel-plated Colt .45. The older man had not even got to his feet.

'The next time you draw on a man, be prepared to get shot,' Jimmy warned him.

'You swindled me, I don't know how but somehow you did it.'

Jimmy shook his head. 'I never cheated you, Billy. I just played against your weaknesses, so let it be a lesson to you.'

Abe laid a strong hand on Billy's shoulder and pushed him down into his chair. 'The man's right. I tried to warn you but you wouldn't listen.'

Jimmy put his gun away, got up from the table and strode towards the bar. He had gone no more than a few steps when he sensed the movement behind him. He crouched, catlike, then spun on the balls of his feet as he swung round. Billy's bullet whizzed past him as his own tore into the boy's heart.

Young Hartigan fell back, dead before his body hit the floor.

Jimmy put the Colt back in its holster. 'I'm sorry I had to do that but he gave me no choice.'

Abe Morgan knelt down by the corpse and gently closed Billy's eyes for the last time. 'Damn you, mister. Why did you have to come here?'

There was no time to answer before a grey-haired man who wore a tin star pinned to his leather waistcoat strode in. He looked down at the body and then more sharply at Jimmy.

'What's gone on here?' he demanded.

'I beat him at cards, he drew on me and I drew first but warned him off. Then, when I turned around he tried to shoot me in the back.'

The sheriff turned to look at the bartender. 'Is that how it was, Joe?'

'It happened just like he said.'

'Anyone got a different story?'

The others stared dumbly at the floor. The sheriff then took Abe Morgan's arm, urging him to his feet.

'I'm sorry, Abe, but everything's square as far as the law's concerned. There's nothing I can do about it.'

'I know, Sheriff, but that don't mean there's nothin' I can do about it' said the ramrod grimly. 'After all, Mr Hartigan will want somethin' done.'

'Let me make one thing clear to everyone,' said the sheriff firmly. 'Whatever scores are going to be settled will be settled away from this town. I want the law kept in Paradise.'

Then he turned towards Jimmy and looked him up and down. 'I don't like your kind. You sharpshooting card men bring trouble wherever you go, so I want you gone by sundown. Is that understood?'

'I thought you said I hadn't broken the law.'

'Well, I could always put you in jail on the grounds that your presence in this town might disturb the peace. How's that, Mr Card Man?'

'The name's Jimmy Casey.'

'Jimmy the Kid, eh? I might have

guessed. Well, I'm Sheriff Ned Hopper and I'm saying that this is your last day in Paradise, so clear out like I told you.'

Jimmy shrugged, knowing better than to argue. 'Whatever you say, Sheriff.'

Hopper placed a hand on Abe Morgan's shoulder. 'I think you'd better take Billy home now,' he said gently.

'How much will it cost to bury him?' asked Jimmy.

'You can keep your money. It won't do you no good, anyway,' Abe told him. He hoisted Billy Hartigan's body onto his broad shoulders and carried it outside.

'You're in deep trouble, Mr Casey,' Joe told him when the others had gone. 'Billy was no good and he got what was coming to him but his old man won't see it that way. Jack Hartigan's men will have orders to track you down and shoot you like a dog, no matter how far you travel. If you kill them, he'll just send more, no matter what it costs.'

'Why doesn't he come after me himself?'

Joe shook his head. 'His legs got trampled by a horse just over ten years ago. He can hardly walk, let alone ride. Abe Morgan took Billy under his wing, taught him how to ride a horse and drive cattle, but the boy was always wild, especially since his mother died. I think Abe knew what Billy was but grew fond of him all the same, probably kept hoping he would grow up someday.'

Jimmy drained the whiskey Joe had just poured him. 'Thanks for the warning. Do you think I'll have time for a bath and a meal before I get going?'

Joe nodded; 'Sure. They'll bury Billy this afternoon and then set off tracking you at first light, I reckon.'

*   *   *

Jimmy planned his next move while in the bath, deciding on a fresh horse to give him a good start, which would

17

mean trading in the palomino. Then, after wolfing down a steak with potatoes, he made his way back to the livery where Clem Bailey still sat puffing on his pipe.

'I hear you shot Billy Hartigan,' the old-timer remarked.

'Not much passes you by in this town, Clem.'

'News like that don't pass nobody by, son. I guess you figure on leavin' pronto, eh?'

'It seems like the smart thing to do but I'll need a fresh horse.'

Clem beamed at him. 'I got just the thing for you.' He led Jimmy into the stable where he pointed to a white stallion standing in one of the stalls. 'That there horse can run like the wind and he's worth eighty dollars.'

'That's a lot of money for a horse.'

'You'll need speed more than money with Jack Hartigan's boys on your trail.'

Jimmy examined the horse closely. He was a truly magnificent animal, alert and nimble as he moved around. He ran a hand along the creature's well muscled flank, looked into his fiery eyes and made up his mind at once.

'I tell you what, Clem. I'll pay fifty dollars plus my palomino. What do you say?'

The old man considered for a moment. 'OK, it's a deal. Your new horse has a name by the way. He's called Banjo.'

Jimmy handed over the money and Clem saddled up the stallion for him. As he cantered off along the street the livery owner called after him with some last words of warning: 'Don't forget to keep lookin' over your shoulder, Jimmy. Hartigan's men are meaner than Lucifer!'

His last stop before leaving town was to buy a rifle at the gunsmith's, and plenty of bullets. Now well-armed and riding a fresh horse, Jimmy left the dust of Paradise behind him as he headed off into the desert towards the Chiricahua Mountains. There was a trading post at Fort Bowie but it would take a couple of days to get there and then another five days to reach Tucson, where Ellen awaited him. He had promised her a wedding day before spring turned to summer. His winnings over the last few months would be enough to give them a good start and at last he was ready to fulfil his promise. It was a year since Jimmy had vowed to stop gambling and cease wandering from town to town in search of easy pickings. Once he had enough money, he told her, he would buy a grocery store and become respectable.

Why did this have to happen now, damn it? He could not risk riding into Tucson with men still on his trail. No, any pursuers would have to be taken care of long before he reached his final destination if he was to ensure that Ellen was not placed in any danger. Besides, a man with killers after him was not a good prospect for any bride and the last thing he wanted was for her to suddenly start having doubts about him.

Jimmy smiled then as he pictured Ellen's smooth, oval face topped with waves of blond hair and the blue eyes that matched his own. He had never quite managed to work out what a sweet, innocent girl like her wanted with an old gambler, but for some strange reason she seemed to love him. It was a love he could not fathom but only return. She made Jimmy want to do what no one else could, to leave his old ways behind and settle down to an ordinary domestic life. Her kindness softened him somehow, but also created a painful awareness of the selfish, aimless life he had led until now. In short, Jimmy wanted to become worthy of the woman who had agreed to marry him.

He rode on as dusk fell, then bedded down under the stars before awaking to a lick from Banjo at first light. He filled his canteen from a nearby gully and checked his weapons before setting off into the dawn. Today was the day he became a hunted man, a man who must

21

run, hide and kill in order to survive. His previous existence had been carefree by comparison. Sheriff Hopper had been right yesterday when he told Jimmy that it was his last day in Paradise.

'Goodbye Paradise,' murmured the gambler, 'and welcome to hell.'

2

When Jack Hartigan was shown the body of his only son, he let out a howl of grief, a sound that Abe Morgan had heard from him just once before, the night his beloved wife died of fever. That loss had embittered and hardened him even more than the crippling accident that followed later. Abe figured that Billy's death would lead to an outpouring of rage as Hartigan's grief became focused on a desire for revenge against the man he held responsible for his loss.

'Tell me, Abe. Who did this to my boy?'

'The man's a gambler and gunslinger called Jimmy Casey.' Abe then described what happened. 'I saw what was comin', boss, and I knew Billy would get mad but I just couldn't get him to see it.'

Hartigan fixed him with the same hard grey eyes he had passed on to his dead son. 'It wasn't your fault, Abe, so there's no call for you to go blamin' yourself. Jimmy Casey made a fool out of Billy and took his money. The boy was bound to get mad, he was a Hartigan after all. Casey should have left him alone and gone someplace else.'

Hartigan ran a hand through his sparse, greying hair. His upper body was still powerful and he used his strong arms to propel his wheelchair closer to the wagon on which his son's body lay under a blanket. The specially adapted vehicle was upholstered in black leather with large iron wheels at each side and a smaller one at the front. A rudder enabled the crippled man to manoeuvre the contraption more easily.

'I swear to you, Billy boy, I'll get the man who did this to you. If I have to sell this place and spend every cent I have, I'll get him!'

The rancher then wheeled himself

over to the men lined up before him. 'I want ten of you, apart from Abe here, to go after this Casey and do to him what he did to Billy. Each man who keeps on Casey's trail until the job's done will get two hundred dollars and there's a bounty of a thousand dollars for whoever shoots him dead, to be shared if it takes more than one of you.'

More than twenty of them volunteered but Jack turned back to Abe. 'You know all these men, so choose the best ones,' he told him. Then he looked down once more at his son's body. 'He was working well, wasn't he? He would have made a fine rancher when the time came for him to take over from me.'

Abe knew better than to tell the old man the truth. 'Yeah, Billy was doin' just fine, boss. He was doin' you proud, just like you always said he would.'

'What did Hopper say about all this?'

'He told Casey to get out of town. He knows he can't stop us from goin' after him but he don't want no trouble in Paradise.'

Jack snorted. 'He won't take my money but at least he don't interfere in things that ain't his concern.'

'Not unless there's a law that says he has to.'

'The goddamn law don't protect nobody, Abe. Money and power does the job every time. Now, get your men together and go after Casey at first light.'

The first streaks of dawn were appearing as Abe Morgan led his men into Paradise to pick up Jimmy's trail. Clem Bailey was already up and about as they rode past. Abe drew to a halt and raised a hand to stop the men behind him.

'Did you see that Casey fella before he left here yesterday?'

The old man shrugged. 'What if I did? I ain't out to help you do Jack Hartigan's dirty work for him.'

Abe smiled wryly. He had always admired Clem's pluck and his refusal to be anything other than his own man. 'I guess you won't mind if I have a look to see what horses you got for sale,' he remarked casually as he dismounted.

Clem said nothing as the ramrod went inside the stables. Abe immediately noticed the empty stall where the white stallion had been, with the palomino in its place. He went outside and got back on his mount. Then, without another word, he led his men out into the desert. He guessed that Casey would be heading towards Fort Bowie but now he knew what horse to look for in the distance.

★   ★   ★

Jimmy was making steady progress across the Arizona basin and eventually reached a trail that led up into the mountains. As he climbed he was surrounded by the tall, thin spires of rock known as hoodoos. They looked like totem poles and lent the area a sinister, haunting appearance. The sun blazed out of a cobalt blue sky that seemed to stretch to infinity above the parched landscape below.

'That's far enough, stranger. Put your hands in the air!'

Jimmy looked around but could see no sign of where the voice came from. Suddenly a bullet whizzed past his ear and he immediately raised his hands. A figure then emerged from the recesses of a cave and Jimmy saw that the man had a rifle trained on him. He was wiry in build and a little shorter than he with black hair and the sallow complexion of a half-breed. As he came closer Jimmy noticed that he seemed nervous and guessed that he was not accustomed to threatening travellers in this way.

'I'm not out to do you any harm,' Jimmy assured him, 'so you can put that gun away and tell me what all this is about.'

'I just don't like bounty hunters,' the man told him.

'I'm no bounty hunter and I can prove it.'

The half-breed was suspicious. 'How?'

he asked but without lowering his gun.

'If I was a bounty hunter I'd have a Wanted poster inside this coat, probably a whole stack of them.'

There was a moment's hesitation before the reply came; 'OK, take off that gunbelt, real slow and then show me that coat.'

Jimmy obeyed slowly, knowing that a nervous adversary holding a rifle could be lethal at point-blank range. The man relaxed slightly as he watched the gunbelt drop to the ground and lowered his weapon as the coat came off. In a flash, Jimmy threw the garment over the fugitive's head and jumped on to him from his horse. He jerked the rifle upwards, directing a shot harmlessly away as he cannoned into his opponent's body, flinging him to the ground. Then, wrenching the rifle out of the man's grasp, he stepped back nimbly.

'It makes you kinda jumpy, having a gun pointed at you, doesn't it?' suggested Jimmy with a smile.

The half-breed stared at the barrel and swallowed hard. 'I wasn't gonna shoot you, mister, honest.'

'Start talking and I'll decide whether to believe you.'

'I was gonna be hanged for a horse-thief, which I'm not, but I managed to escape. Some of my mother's people live on a reservation around here and I figured I could hide out there. I saw you following and thought you must be after me.'

'I wasn't following you. In fact there are some very unpleasant people after me on account of my having shot someone in self-defence. It turns out the young man's pa is rich and powerful.' Jimmy lowered the gun. 'Come on, get up. What's your name?'

'Officially, I'm Tom Taylor but I'm also known as Tom Tames Horses.'

'What kind of a name is that?'

'My mother was a Chiricahua Apache. She gave it to me because I'm good with horses, but my father's name was

Taylor and I usually stick with that.'

'Have you got a horse?'

'Yeah, he's in the cave.'

'Well, I'm Jimmy Casey. If you don't mind me riding along with you we'll head for that reservation of yours. I could do with a place to hide myself.'

'Sure, I reckon it's the least I can do after giving you such a scare.'

Tom dusted himself down and went to fetch his mount, which turned out to be a magnificent pinto, brown with white patches. The two of them set off and gradually Jimmy learned more details of his companion's story. It turned out that he was the intended victim of a Texas lynch mob who tried him in a makeshift court set up in a saloon without a proper judge. A few horses had been stolen and, in some men's eyes, Indian blood combined with good horsemanship rendered a man guilty. Led by their bigoted sheriff, the townspeople quickly made up their minds and Tom's fate appeared sealed. Fortunately, the sheriff's daughter had none of her father's prejudices and smuggled a key to him in his cell, hidden in the contents of what was intended to be his last meal.

'Did they send a posse after you?'

'Yeah, I was followed for three days but managed to outrun them.'

'Well, I don't think you need to worry about bounty hunters. They only go for men who've got a definite price on their heads, not innocents who escaped a lynching.'

'I'm not used to this sort of thing. I was a store clerk before I went on the run.'

'Well, if those men catch up with me you just make a run for it,' Jimmy told him. 'It's not your fight and you've had enough trouble already.'

Tom shook his head vigorously. 'No way. I can shoot and I can ride fast. You didn't kill me when you had good reason to, so I reckon I owe you.'

Jimmy's reply died in his throat when he saw that the path ahead was blocked by a group of five Apache warriors.

They sat, proud and erect in their horses' saddles, each man holding a tall spear but also armed with a rifle. The travellers kept still as the Apaches encircled them. Then, suddenly, Tom spoke to them in their own language. The warriors halted, surprised, and then the man who appeared to be their leader replied, his tone cautious. Jimmy waited while the conversation continued and the atmosphere slowly grew less tense. Then there were smiles and one of the Apaches addressed Jimmy in English.

'You are a friend of Tames Horses and so a friend of the Apache. We shall ride with you and keep you safe.'

Jimmy tipped his hat to his new friends. 'I'm much obliged,' he said nonchalantly, and their journey continued. While they climbed higher into the mountains, Tom explained that the Chiricahua Apaches were finding it difficult to survive on their reservation and the fragile peace was now under threat as they had begun to attack

33

travellers and carry out raids in order to obtain more supplies. Their own lucky escape had been due to Tom's ability to speak their language, his Apache descent and the fact that distant relatives of his were currently living on the reservation. They had not gone much further, however, when one of the warriors turned and pointed below them to a rapidly approaching cloud of dust. It looked as though Jimmy's pursuers were starting to catch up.

★ ★ ★

Abe Morgan had spotted the fugitives and their new friends through his spyglass. 'It looks like we got more than we bargained for,' he said drily and described what he had seen.

'Mr Hartigan never said nothin' about Apaches,' said Hal Hollister warily. He was an old army man who had encountered them before and had a jagged scar across his right cheek to prove it.

'He never said this would be easy neither. What do you think you're being paid for?' Abe shut the spyglass and led his men forward, ignoring their grumbles about the odds they faced. They still out-numbered Casey and his companions, after all.

One of the Apaches, an older man who appeared to have some authority over his companions, ordered them to dismount and then sent three of them further on ahead to a point where they began to climb down. The trio quickly disappeared from view and Jimmy looked questioningly at Tom.

'Apache warriors can run faster than a horse when they have to and move without being seen. Those three men will skirt around behind your enemies while we defend against attack from the front.'

Jimmy dismounted and settled himself behind a large rock before checking his rifle. Tom and the remaining two Apaches spread themselves further along a line of hoodoos which provided some cover.

Abe ordered his men to spread out as they came within range and Jimmy narrowly missed one of them with his first shot. A second later, however, Hal Hollister tumbled from his horse as an Apache arrow embedded itself in his throat. Another of Abe's companions was hit squarely in the chest by Jimmy's second bullet and was dead before he hit the ground. A third man died when an arrow pierced his jugular vein. By now, however, Jimmy's assailants had reached the shelter of some rocks lower down. They dismounted and were returning heavy fire. The warrior next to Tom was hit in the stomach as he hurled his lance; he slumped forward, his weapon clattering harmlessly to the ground.

The two sides now had each other pinned down and rapidly exchanged fire. At the rocks below Abe heard a choked cry from behind and turned to see another of his men fall dead, this one with an Apache knife stuck between his shoulder blades. Rolling quickly on to his back, he fired at the warrior who had thrown it, killing him instantly. A second Apache leaped at him with a club and he rolled again, so that it swung past his temple. As he raised his gun to fire, he heard a shot and his attacker crumpled to the ground. Looking up, he saw that the shooter was Jay Hickock, one of his best men. He was too late to shout a warning as a third Apache appeared from behind and slit Hickock's throat. Abe fired once more and the Apache staggered a few steps before falling face down in the dirt.

'That's five men we've lost, damn it,' muttered Walt Simmons as he crawled forward to take up a position next to Abe. Walt had worked for Jack Hartigan almost as long as Abe himself. He had sunburned, hawkish features and a beard that was heavily salted with grey. 'Still, I guess they've lost four of their own,' he added before reloading his rifle.

'Maybe me and a couple of the boys could work our way in closer by that cactus over to the right there,' Abe told him.

'Go on, we'll cover you,' said Walt, signalling to two of the men further to their left who now began shooting in earnest. Abe scurried away towards the two men he had in mind, dodging behind rocks and boulders as bullets flew around him.

Lodged on the escarpment above, Jimmy saw what Abe was up to and responded with a hail of bullets. Then, cursing, he threw the rifle aside and drew out his pistols. As he got up to go Tom laid a hand on his arm and asked what he was doing.

'I'm going to cut those three off before they reach us. You stay here with our Apache friend and keep the others pinned down.'

Keeping his body low, Jimmy made his way about a hundred yards over to the right where there was a large boulder and a bend in the path just beyond it. Below that stood the cactus plant that Abe had spotted. He dodged behind the boulder and waited tensely. Then, between the sporadic bursts of gunfire, he heard a faint scrabbling and the jingle of spurs. Taking a deep breath, Jimmy leaped from his hiding place and fired both guns rapidly while still in mid air. Abe's two companions were both riddled with bullets and by the time their leader returned fire Jimmy had landed and rolled safely behind the cover of some rocks lower down. Cursing, Abe ducked down low and retreated back the way he had come.

'You won't get away from me, Casey. Run as far and as fast as you want, I'll just keep on comin' after you!'

Jimmy shivered as he heard Abe's parting words, but at that moment the sound of a trumpet blast rent the air and a cavalry troop came into view, led by a young officer. The soldiers halted by Abe and his remaining men and Jimmy watched as they exchanged words. He returned to join Tom and the older Apache, who was now anxious for them to leave.

'Running Bear says we must leave now and return to the reservation. The soldiers must not find him out here. Come, he knows a path where we will not be followed.'

Jimmy agreed readily. He realized that Abe Morgan and his followers would now go to Fort Bowie with the cavalry before trying to pick up his trail again. Hiding out at the reservation for a day or two would help him to evade them and reach the fort after they had left. Then he would track his pursuers and allow the hunters to become the hunted.

The young officer introduced himself as Lieutenant William Ross. Abe judged him to be in his early twenties and probably a West Point graduate with limited experience of fighting Apaches.

'I'm afraid the Chiricahua Apaches have been hostile lately, attacking travellers and wagon trains, but we're doing our best to control the situation,' the young man told him.

'I'm sure you are, Lieutenant. It

looks like you scared the rest of them off, anyway,' replied Abe in a friendly tone. The last thing he wanted was for these soldiers to go poking around in the hills and find Casey, who would be only too happy to point out who the real aggressors were.

'We've been out here on patrol but we're heading back to Fort Bowie now. If you'd like to come with us, we'd be more than happy to offer you our protection.'

Abe was not sure how useful the kid himself would be in a fight but he had plenty of men and if there was a risk of running into more Indians then it was probably best to play along for now.

'Thanks, Lieutenant, we'd be very grateful.' Apart from his old friend Walt, he now had only two men left. Hank Whitworth was a taciturn man, tall and lean, but reliable when there was a job to be done. Like a lot of men who had been through the war, he had grown used to killing when he had to and was not particularly squeamish about it.

Guy Dolman was younger, fast with a gun but also quick tempered and impetuous. Perhaps not the best man to bring along, but he reminded Abe of Billy and why they were out here.

The four civilians fell in behind the troops and headed off towards Fort Bowie while Jimmy and his two remaining companions watched from a distance. The reservation was near the fort but Running Bear led them along a circuitous route through a winding mountain pass. They had to go on foot part of the way, leading their horses but Banjo was nimble as well as fast and made few snorts of complaint. They made camp at dusk but decided not to risk a fire and were off again at dawn after a cold night on hard ground.

They reached their destination that afternoon, a desolate stretch of land upon which the Chiricahua Apaches struggled to maintain their traditional way of life as best they could. Jimmy took in the mass of tepees, the old women hunched over their cooking fires and the despair etched on the faces of the young men marooned in a land where there were no buffalo to hunt and very little to eat. There were a few huts and adobe buildings, presumably for the administrators who ran the place, but little else apart from the mission school and the spire of a plain wooden church.

Tom pointed to the vegetable patches scattered about. 'These people are not farmers and the soil is too poor for them to be able to grow much. They live on supplies brought in from outside. No wonder some of them prefer to steal.'

Running Bear led them to his own tepee where he had lived alone since the death of his wife. As a white man, Jimmy attracted some strange looks from the inhabitants but, seeing that he was in the company of a respected elder of the tribe, none said a word. Tom went off in search of his relatives while Jimmy sat with Running Bear, who prepared a stew consisting of beans and some root vegetables for their supper.

Tom returned a short time later, having discovered that the two cousins he had come in search of had both died. One was killed in a skirmish with prospectors and the other, a young woman, succumbed to disease. 'There's nothing for me here, I'll leave tomorrow,' he declared.

'Didn't you find anyone you knew?' Jimmy asked him.

'There's a warrior here called Walks Softly. He was married to my female cousin and is very angry about what has happened to his people. We talked for a while but even he said that there is no point in staying.'

'Well, it will be dangerous for you to stick with me,' warned Jimmy.

Tom shrugged. 'Those men who are after you killed some of my friends. That makes them my enemies too.'

Jimmy unpacked his bedroll while Running Bear entertained them with a song extolling his ancestors' exploits. Tom translated the words for him but it was the low, humming rhythm that he enjoyed, finding it strangely comforting. An orange sunset faded into black as night fell, the stars tiny pinpricks of light far above them. They slept heavily, Jimmy wondering what his pursuers were up to as he drifted off to sleep.

3

Abe Morgan and his companions reached Fort Bowie at noon that day. The place had been rebuilt two years previously on a plateau near the original site. It now consisted of a series of rectangular adobe barracks, corrals for cavalry horses, a trading post, a hospital and a few houses including some accommodation for travellers. After seeing to their horses, Abe and his men went straight to the trading post to get fresh supplies. As he stepped across the threshold he was surprised to see a young blonde woman, obviously travelling alone, gather up her purchases. Her buckskin riding outfit did not look particularly worn and he guessed that she was not a seasoned traveller, especially when he heard her ask if there were any maps of the area more detailed than the one she had.

'Excuse me, miss, I don't aim to boast, but I know this territory real well. If you need help findin' your way, I'd gladly be of service.'

The woman turned and he found himself dazzled by her smile. Her eyes were an oceanic blue, a colour he had seen only once before in his life when he rode by the Gulf of Mexico. He had not expected to find it here.

'Why, that's very kind of you 'Mr . . . ?'

'The name's Abe Morgan,' he replied, stumbling over the words as he removed his hat. 'These gentlemen here are Walt Simmons, Hank Whitworth and Guy Dolman.'

'I'm Ellen Garrett. I came here from Tucson with a wagon train but now I have to strike out on my own to get to the nearest town. I understand it's called Paradise, is that right?'

For a moment, Abe was distracted by the soft, warm tone of her voice but quickly recovered himself. 'Yeah, we're all from a ranch just a couple of miles outside it. Paradise is about two days' ride from here but you don't want to be goin' there all by yourself.'

'Why ever not?' she asked, her eyes widening in surprise.

'This whole territory's crawlin' with Indians,' Walt Simmons informed her.

'He's right, Miss Garrett,' added Abe. 'In fact, we were attacked ourselves on the way here and most of my men were killed. Fortunately, the cavalry turned up just after that.'

Ellen Garrett placed a small gloved hand over her widely opened mouth. 'Oh, that's terrible. I'm so sorry, Mr Morgan.' She placed another hand comfortingly on his arm.

'So you see, Miss Garrett, we couldn't possibly allow you to travel to Paradise alone. Now, we've some business to attend to further north but once we return in a few days you can come to Paradise with us. How does that sound?'

'Oh, you're very kind, Mr Morgan and I'd love to accept your offer, but I really can't afford to wait that long. You see, I'm looking for someone, only he doesn't know I am, and if he's in Paradise I don't want him to leave before I get there.' Ellen Garrett gabbled these last words as her features contorted into a frown of anxiety.

'Oh I'm sure you'll find him, Miss Garrett,' Abe told her reassuringly. 'There aren't many places in these parts where a man can go. How certain are you that he went to Paradise?'

'To tell you the truth I don't know where he went but that's the nearest place he could be, isn't it?'

'Sure it is, but it just ain't safe for you to go there by yourself, that's all,' Walt reminded her.

Suddenly the young woman dissolved into tears. 'Oh it's hopeless!' she wailed. 'Even if he is in Paradise, he'll have gone by the time I get there.'

Abe quickly guided her to a stool and sat her down while his companions shuffled awkwardly behind him. 'Come on now, Miss Garrett, it can't be as bad as all that. Why don't just tell me all about it?' he urged her.

'You'll think me a terrible fool, Mr Morgan but the man I've chosen as my future husband is a gambler. He goes from town to town in Texas and Arizona, looking for card games. This is his last trip but I just got tired of waiting for him to come home. I came out here myself to find him. I was going to tell him that he's got to come back right now so we can get married, but if I can't find him, what's the use?'

The truth was slowly dawning on Abe and his companions and they exchanged looks. The young woman raised her tear-stained face to look up at them, suddenly fearful at the grave expressions that confronted her.

'Now, what's this fellow's name?' Abe asked her.

'Jimmy Casey.'

Abe feigned a look of surprise. 'Really? Well, it just so happens that a gambling man by that name rolled into town just as we were leaving. Dry your tears, Miss Garrett. Our business can wait. First thing tomorrow we'll take you back to Paradise with us.'

'Oh, thank you so much, all of you. I don't know what to say.'

'There's no need to say anything. Now, if Jimmy's not there when we get back, we'll be sure to find out where he's gone and pick up his trail so we can find him again. You must leave a note here for him to say that you've gone to Paradise with us in search of him. All travellers in these parts pass by here at some point and stop to pick up supplies so he's bound to get it.'

Ellen Garrett quickly composed herself and got to her feet, beaming with joy. 'Mr Morgan, thank you so much, you and your friends here.' She got out a notebook and hastily scribbled a brief letter, which she placed in an envelope and wrote Jimmy's name on the front. The trader was given a detailed description of him and assured her that he would deliver the note if Jimmy turned up there in the future.

'If I was Jimmy Casey, Miss Garrett, you wouldn't need to come chasin' after me when I'd you to come home to,' Abe told her as he went to open the door before her departure. She blushed at that but said nothing as she went off to get some rest. He then handed the trader a dollar bill, just to make sure he remembered the note.

Once they had bought their provisions and were back outside Walt Simmons congratulated Abe on his foresight. 'I gotta hand it to you, Abe. Casey's bound to go plumb crazy when he gets that note and realizes we've got his girl. He'll follow us back to Paradise but he won't do a thing, knowin' that she's our hostage.'

'That's right,' added Hank Whitworth. 'It'll be easy to get Casey to just come to us unarmed if he's as sweet on her as she is on him.'

'Let's get one thing straight. Miss Garrett isn't to be harmed in any way and she isn't to find out she's a hostage or what we're gonna do until she has to.'

'Sure, Abe,' replied Guy Dolman, 'but you'll let us have our fun afterwards, won't you? I hope you ain't figurin' on keepin' that gal all to yourself.'

The vehemence of Abe's reaction startled all of them. 'Goddamn you! I'll shoot the first man who so much as looks at her the wrong way. Do you hear me?'

Guy backed off and smoothed down his rumpled clothes as Abe released his grip. 'You're the boss, whatever you say,' he replied.

'Good, just don't you forget it.'

*   *   *

Jimmy opened the flap of Running Bear's tepee as dawn broke over the reservation. He stood and watched the rising sun for a few moments before going to fetch some coffee and beans for breakfast from his saddle-bag. Tom was up on his return, while Running Bear remained asleep. As they sat over their breakfast a cavalry troop rode past, headed by the same officer they had seen the previous day. He drew his men to a halt alongside them.

'I'm Lieutenant Ross. I don't know what you gentlemen are doing here but it's a dangerous place for you to be right now. Some Indians attacked a group of travellers yesterday and killed seven men. I mean to find the culprits and make an example of them.'

Jimmy looked up at the young man and appraised him coolly. 'I'm Jimmy Casey and this is Tom Taylor. Maybe you ought to get your facts straight before you go around taking reprisals, Lieutenant.'

'What do you mean? I saw the incident for myself.'

'Those men you picked up yesterday were after me because I killed one of their friends in self defence. The dead Apaches you saw died defending me against them.'

'I never heard of Apaches defending a white man,' said Ross.

'I guess if I hadn't run into Tom here, who speaks their language, they might have figured it was none of their business and I'd have been outnumbered ten to one. Fortunately, he persuaded them to help.'

'Everything he says is true. I was riding with him when it happened,' added Tom.

Ross hesitated for a moment but then quickly asserted his authority. 'Those Apaches shouldn't have left the reservation. They must have been on a raid, so I'm still going to have to . . . ' Ross paused as Running Bear came out of his tepee and stood squarely in front of him. He spoke pointedly to Ross, then folded his arms across his chest.

Tom translated the old man's words: 'I understand your language but will not speak it. Why do you not believe this white man when he speaks the truth? Is it because white men lie to each other and not just to the Apache, or is it because you choose only to believe what is spoken against us?'

As Ross hesitated once more, Jimmy urged him to leave. 'Look, Lieutenant, it wouldn't go down too well in a court of inquiry or with the newspapers back East if your men gunned down Apaches for saving a man's life. I suggest you just turn around and ride along out of here like nothing ever happened.'

'I'll still be making a report about yesterday's incident, Mr Casey, so I hope all you've told me is accurate,' said Ross self-importantly, before turning to lead his men out.

'Run along and make your report, little soldier boy,' muttered Jimmy to the lieutenant's retreating back as he threw the remains of his coffee on the fire.

'Come on, we'd best get going ourselves,' said Tom.

They took their leave of Running Bear and rode off in the direction the troops had taken, arriving at Fort Bowie later that morning. They made straight for the trading post to stock up on food and ammunition. As Jimmy paid his bill, the man behind the counter asked his name, then handed him an envelope. He tore it open, quickly scanned its contents, then paled visibly.

'What's wrong?' Tom asked.

'It's Morgan and his men. They've got my girl.'

'How can that have happened? I don't understand.'

'According to this note, she came out here to look for me and ran into Abe Morgan and three of his men. She's gone with them to Paradise to look for me.'

'Does Morgan know who she is?'

'Of course he does,' replied Jimmy bitterly. 'He's using Ellen as bait and he won't release her until I surrender, maybe not even then.' He turned back to the trader to ask when Ellen had left.

'I didn't see her go but she said she was gonna leave with them fellas first thing this mornin', as I recall.'

'This could be dangerous for you, Tom. We'll go our separate ways now.'

'No, Jimmy. I agreed to help you and that means sticking with you all the way. Besides, I can't ignore a woman in need of help, can I?'

Jimmy was genuinely moved by his friend's loyalty. 'I guess not. Thanks, Tom, I really appreciate it.'

Soon they were on their way again, heading back towards Paradise. They picked up the trail of five riders, heading in the same direction they were going. Jimmy knew that Abe had three men left so the numbers matched. Tom squatted on the ground and examined the hoofprints more closely.

'These are quite fresh, so I'd say we're only a few hours behind.'

Jimmy squinted through his spyglass and spotted tiny figures in the distance. He passed it to his companion. 'What do you make of that?'

'Yeah, I think it could be them. If we go just a little faster we should catch up well before sundown. After all, they want us to catch up, don't they?'

They set a brisk pace but were

careful not to over-tire their horses. A man on foot was often a dead man in this desert. As the day wore on, they reached a watering hole which Jimmy recalled having used on his way from Paradise to Fort Bowie. As they watered the horses and refilled their canteens Tom examined some tracks he had found.

'They were here, maybe an hour ago, I'd say.'

Jimmy peered once more through the spyglass. 'Yeah, it's them all right.' he said grimly, swallowing hard as he made out Ellen's tiny figure. 'We need to skirt around them somehow, find some higher ground if we can.'

Tom frowned as he scanned the surrounding landscape, then pointed over to their left. 'We could make for that canyon over there. It sweeps around in the direction they're going, but we may lose some time.'

'That might not be a bad thing, coming upon them at dusk. With luck, we should be able to give our friends a surprise.'

'What are you going to do?'

Jimmy smiled grimly. 'You'll see. You wouldn't want me to spoil the surprise now, would you?'

⋆　⋆　⋆

Ahead of their pursuers Abe and his men were making steady progress. Ellen found the journey hard but did not like to complain. After all, they had already had a brief rest at the watering hole not much over an hour ago.

'We could stop for a while if you're tired,' suggested Abe as he dropped back to trot beside her.

'Oh, I'm fine. Besides, I don't want to hold you up when you're all going to such trouble on my account.'

'It's no trouble. Anyhow, we didn't stop for long last time and I figure the horses could do with a rest too.'

He called to his companions to signal that they were stopping and loosened the reins of his horse. Ellen dismounted and sat down beneath the shade of a nearby stretch of overhanging rock. Abe came and joined her.

'Miss Garrett, there's somethin' been on my mind that I think I ought to tell you about. It concerns your friend Mr Casey.'

Ellen felt suddenly alarmed. 'What is it? I thought you only saw Jimmy arrive as you were leaving.'

'Well, that ain't strictly true,' he said awkwardly. 'You see, I didn't like to mention this before, on account of him bein' your sweetheart an' all . . . '

'Please, Mr Morgan. If you've some bad news about Jimmy I'd rather you came straight out with it. Has he been hurt?'

Abe shook his head. 'No, but I'm afraid he killed a man. In fact, the fella he shot was barely a man at all, just a boy really.'

Ellen shook her head from side to side, unable to believe what she was hearing. Jimmy was no killer, but she could not imagine why this seemingly kind man would invent such a thing.

'Can you tell me exactly what happened?'

'Well, Billy Hartigan, a fine young man I've known since he was a boy, had a game of poker goin' in our saloon when in walked your Mr Casey and asked if he could join in. Anyway, they got down to playin' and Billy won the first round, but I figured at the time that Mr Casey let him win. Then in the next round he got Billy to bet all his winnings, which Mr Casey won on account of havin' the best hand.' Abe paused and looked up at this point to see what effect his story was having.

'What happened next?'

'Well, Billy got mad. I guess he figured Mr Casey cheated him somehow, which I don't reckon he did. Anyhow, there was a gunfight and Mr Casey shot Billy dead.'

'This man Billy Hartigan drew first though, didn't he?' asked Ellen.

'That's true, Miss Garrett and I'm sure Mr Casey weren't no cheat neither . . . but . . . it's just . . . ' Abe allowed his voice to trail away and then waited.

'What is it, Mr Morgan? Please tell me.'

'Well, it seems to me that when a professional gambler takes advantage of a young boy's youth and inexperience, it's no surprise if the boy gets mad and pulls a gun on him. I figure he could have shot the gun out of his hand, or aimed low or somethin' like that.'

Ellen looked down, feeling suddenly shocked and ashamed. 'Thank you for telling me this, Mr Morgan. I appreciate how difficult it was for you.'

'Well, to tell you the truth, Miss Garrett, I couldn't have lived with myself if I hadn't have told you. I mean, I have to ask myself if a fine young lady like you really wants to marry a man who takes advantage of a boy's foolishness and then shoots him dead over a card game.'

'When you put it like that, Mr Morgan, I guess the answer is that I don't.'

Walt Simmons overheard enough of

the conversation to feel worried. As Abe passed him to tend to his horse, his old friend seized his arm. 'What in hell's name are you tryin' to do?' he hissed.

'Nothin' you need to concern yourself with,' replied Abe, shrugging off Walt's grip.

'I got eyes in my head, Abe. I can see you've taken a shine to that girl, but don't forget we've a job to do, a job she ain't gonna like one bit.'

'I ain't forgotten, Walt. I aim to turn her against him, get her to see Casey's no good and then I'll give him a chance to attack us. She'll see things differently when we shoot him defendin' ourselves.'

Walt shook his head as Abe walked away from him. Hank Whitworth approached him from behind. He too had observed their boss's attentiveness towards Ellen Garrett.

'That sounded like trouble to me,' Hank observed drily as he lit a cigar.

'Yeah, there ain't no fool bigger than a man who fools himself over a woman.'

Their conversation was interrupted by the sound of screaming and both men turned to see Ellen struggling against the embraces of Guy Dolman.

'Aw, come on, missy. There's no harm in just one little kiss, is there?'

Ellen tried vainly to push him away as Guy pressed his mouth down hard upon hers. Then a large hand seized his shoulder and spun him around. Abe's fist smashed into the younger man's jaw and Guy was sent sprawling on to the ground. As he sat up and wiped a trickle of blood from the corner of his mouth, Abe shot him a brief look of contempt before turning away. Steel flashed in the sunlight as Guy drew out his knife and sprang at his attacker, but Abe had sensed the movement even before he heard Walt's cry of warning. Guy found his wrist and elbow held in a vicelike grip before he was flung once more to the ground and held there with a knee pressed hard against his chest.

'What are you makin' such a fuss for? You can get better than her in any two-bit whorehouse,' cried his young foe defiantly.

Abe was now possessed by a blind fury. Grabbing a nearby rock, he raised his arm and brought the object crashing down upon Guy's skull, again and again. Walt and Hank tried to drag him away but Abe's rage seemed to confer on him an almost superhuman strength and he was able to strike twice more before they pulled him off. Suddenly, his anger subsided and he looked with horror at the bloodied rock in his hand before dropping it.

Walt bent down over Guy's inert form and examined the side of the young man's head where the skull had almost completely caved in. Then he straightened up, shaking his head sadly. Abe turned and looked pleadingly at Ellen Garrett, who was sobbing in shock and terror at what she had just witnessed.

'I couldn't let him treat you like that, Miss Garrett, I just couldn't. You understand that, don't you? I didn't mean to kill nobody but a man's gotta defend a lady's honour.'

Ellen stumbled to her feet and ran over to the horses. She was about to place her foot in the stirrup when strong arms grabbed her from behind and spun her around. She found herself gazing into the cold, hard eyes of Hank Whitworth.

'Sorry, darlin', but you ain't goin' nowhere,' he told her.

'What do you mean? Let me go at once!'

Hank shook his head. 'I can't do that, lady. You see, Jimmy Casey shot the son of a rich man and I've got a thousand dollars comin' to me if I put a bullet in him. As long as you're with us, he'll be sure to catch up.'

Slowly, the truth dawned on Ellen Garrett. These men were hired killers hunting a man who, she now realized, was her only hope of rescue and whom she never should have doubted. Walt came over to join them and smiled apologetically as he held up a length of rope.

'I'm afraid we'll have to tie you to that horse. We can't have you runnin' off now, can we, miss?'

'Just tell me one thing. What really happened in Paradise?'

'Billy was a spoiled young pup who didn't play fair and Jimmy taught him a lesson. When Billy pulled a gun, Jimmy warned him off, but then Billy went to shoot him in the back. I guess your fella didn't have much choice about what he did but Jack Hartigan don't see it that way. Besides, Abe was very fond of young Billy, in spite of what he was. I guess I was too, come to that and we're gettin' paid good money to put Jimmy Casey in the ground.'

'Thanks, that's all I wanted to know,' she said as he tightened her bonds.

4

Jimmy noticed the buzzards circling overhead and peered at them through his spyglass as they settled on Guy Dolman's corpse. He wasted no time pondering over what had happened, however. The most important thing now was to catch up with his enemies before they harmed Ellen.

'It looks like Morgan has only two men left. That should improve the odds a little in our favour, don't you think?' He passed the spyglass to Tom who shook his head after taking a brief look.

'If they've started fighting among themselves, it means they're edgy and maybe more dangerous. We'd best be careful.'

Jimmy nodded. 'Sure, but men in that state make mistakes. They don't think straight and that's what I'm counting on.'

They kept up a steady pace and soon reached the canyon where they climbed higher between the surrounding walls of rock. The incline was steep as they headed for higher ground but at least there was some shade from the blistering heat of the sun and the air was cooler. As dusk drew near, they dropped down on to a plateau of rock above the desert basin.

Tom looked over the edge, then put a finger to his lips while signalling that their quarry had camped just below them. Earlier, they had taken the precaution of wrapping their horses' hoofs with strips of cloth and walking them slowly to deaden the sound of their approach. Jimmy was now quite confident that Abe Morgan and his men had no idea that there was anyone above them. His years of gambling had taught him patience and he put that virtue to use as he settled down to wait.

Down below, Walt Simmons was cooking up some beans and dried beef for supper. Hank came over and poured himself some coffee before glancing over at their hostage. Ellen had lapsed into a sullen silence which suited him just fine. The last thing he wanted to hear was the voice of a woman complaining. Abe sat morosely on a rock, brooding on his folly. He knew that his infatuation had brought him nothing but trouble, leading him to kill one of his men and lose the respect of the others. To make things even worse, the object of his affection could not bear to look at him and shuddered at his approach.

'Is Abe still feelin' sorry for himself?' asked Walt as he stirred the pot.

'It looks that way, but the girl ain't givin' no trouble.'

'Well, that's somethin' I guess.' Walt passed Hank a plate of food and spooned the rest on to tin plates. He offered one to Ellen who shook her head listlessly.

'Come on, there's no sense in starvin' yourself. That won't do nobody no good,' he said, shoving a spoon into her hand. She shrugged and began to eat reluctantly, her bound wrists making the task somewhat laborious.

Abe took a swig from the bottle of whiskey he carried for medicinal purposes, alcohol being a good disinfectant and anaesthetic if a man picked up an injury out here in the desert. He was not used to regular drinking and his speech was slightly slurred as he pushed away the plate Walt dropped in front of him.

'Gimme that,' said Walt angrily, he grabbed the bottle and smashed it against a nearby rock. Abe stumbled to his feet and made ready to strike but his friend pushed him back down again.

'This ain't no way to carry on. You'd best pull yourself together if we're to finish our job. Jack Hartigan won't be too pleased if we let him down and old Jack's dependin' on you most of all.'

Abe slowly took in the older man's words and saw the sense in them. He wasn't the first man to go crazy over a woman and he wouldn't be the last.

Now it was over and he had to get a grip on himself. He hauled himself to his feet and straightened his clothing.

'Hank, you take the first watch. Wake me in a couple of hours when I'll have sobered up. Walt, you can go last.'

'Whatever you say, boss,' said Walt, allowing himself a smile. Things were finally getting back to normal. That Guy Dolman was no good anyway: nothing but trouble.

* * *

A pale moon hovered over the Chiricahua mountains as Jimmy withdrew the knife he habitually carried inside the top of his right boot. It had a distinctive handle, carved in the shape of a fish, and he knew that Ellen would recognize it. Holding the blade between his teeth, he began a slow descent to the ground below.

Walt sat by the dying embers of the fire, a blanket around his shoulders. In a couple of hours the first light of dawn would be visible but for now all was quiet as his companions slept. Suddenly he tensed, aware of something behind him, and his fingers tightened around the rifle that lay across his knees. A hand muffled the shout that was about to emerge from his lips as the blade slid expertly between his ribs.

Jimmy gently laid his victim down upon the ground, then crept over to where Abe slept, carefully placing the knife beside him. He was tempted to wake Ellen, cut her bonds and take her with him, but that would risk discovery and the death of both of them. He doubted that it was possible to free her without alerting her captors. No, he decided, it was best to stick to his original plan. Reluctantly, he slipped away and began his ascent to the plateau above.

Hank awoke first as the inky blackness of night faded into the dim grey light of dawn. He stood up and stretched before strolling over to where Walt lay upon the ground. He assumed that his companion had fallen asleep and was startled by the blood that pooled around his feet as he leaned over him. Then he looked into the unseeing eyes and saw the look of alarm frozen on the dead man's face. Turning around, he saw the bloody knife lying beside Abe Morgan. Angrily he kicked the other man awake.

'Goddamn you! What in hell made you do that?' he demanded, pointing at Walt's body just a few feet away.

Abe looked in horror at what had happened and then at the knife beside him. He shook his head vigorously. 'Twenty years I knew Walt Simmons. He was one of the best friends I ever had. Whoever did this to him, it weren't me.'

'I saw you argue with Walt only last evenin' and you already killed Guy. Besides, how did that knife get there?'

'Have you ever seen me with that knife before?'

'No, I ain't never seen it before.'

'Don't you think if I killed him I'd

have the sense to hide it?'

Hank considered this for a moment. 'Well, with the crazy way you've been actin' lately, what am I supposed to think?'

'I guess whoever killed Walt figured that way too.'

Suddenly Hank's jaw tightened. 'Casey must have been hidin' up there some place. He came down in the night, stabbed Walt and hoped maybe we'd fight and one of us would kill the other.' He picked up the knife and strode over to where Ellen huddled against a boulder, trying not to look at the dead man. Hank waved the weapon in her face.

'This is his knife, isn't it?'

She remained silent, cowering as he shook her roughly. 'It won't do you no good to deny it. I know it was him but he ain't gonna get me.' Then he hauled Ellen to her feet and turned to face the canyon, holding the knife to her throat as he did so.

'Come and get her, Casey! Come on if you dare!' shouted Hank, his voice echoing against the wall of rock in front of him.

'Now you're the one actin' crazy,' Abe admonished him. 'Casey wants you to lose your nerve but we have to stay calm. He won't come if he thinks we're ready for him.'

'I guess you're right,' conceded Hank reluctantly as he pushed the girl away from him, tossing the knife on the ground as he did so.

'That's better. Now, let's get her sat between us while we have some breakfast. If Casey's up there, he won't try to shoot at us in case he hits his girl.'

★ ★ ★

High above them Jimmy and Tom watched the scene intently. 'Things didn't quite work out how you planned,' observed Tom.

'I guess not, but at least now there are only two of them. We'll just keep following and see what happens.'

'I hope you don't plan on giving yourself up.'

Jimmy shook his head. 'There's no guarantee they'd let Ellen go if I did. She'd be a witness to my death and they won't want to risk a warrant for murder.'

They watched as Abe and Hank packed away their things, put Ellen back on her horse and led her off into the desert towards Paradise which, by Jimmy's reckoning, they would reach at around noon the next day. Tom suggested that they give their enemies an hour's start and then pick up their trail, since this would allow him and Jimmy to remain out of sight. This was agreed and the two of them settled down to an uneasy wait.

★   ★   ★

Ellen Garrett slumped wearily in the saddle as the heat of the day grew more intense. The sight of the fish-handled knife had ignited a flame of hope inside her, however. Jimmy was following and she knew that he would do all in his power to rescue her from these desperate men, even at the cost of his own life. Even so, she could make it easier for him by at least making some effort to save herself. Hank had not seen her cover the knife with her body when he dropped it before pushing her away from him. By the time she was hauled to her feet again it had been hidden safely inside her blouse. Slowly, she reached for it with her fingers and began to slice through the rope that bound her wrists together.

Up ahead, Hank and Abe rode alongside one another. Ellen looked up and saw that they were engrossed in conversation. Taking a deep breath, she cut through the rope which bound her mount to Hank's, wheeled around and dug her heels into the horse's flanks, speeding back the way they had come. She prayed that Jimmy was not too far away and that she would stay ahead of pursuit long enough to reach him.

Hank swore loudly as the rope went slack and whipped a rifle from his saddle-bag. Abe angrily wrenched the barrel away from him as he raised the weapon to take aim.

'Goddamn it! She's no use to us dead and if she's wounded she'll only slow us down. Come on, let's get after her.'

The two men set off in pursuit and quickly gained on their quarry. Ellen glanced behind her anxiously and spurred her horse on to go faster. The distance between her and her captors widened again but only slightly. Abe and Hank now spread out in an effort to outflank her movement, as they started to catch up once more. Ellen could feel her horse tiring as the chase continued, the poor creature's breath coming in snorts as sweat ran down his flanks. Hank had drawn away from Abe and was getting closer.

Then, suddenly, her horse stumbled and fell. Ellen was thrown clear but tumbled down a sandy slope. Bruised but unhurt, she jumped to her feet and saw with horror that Abe was bearing down on her, though his progress was slowed as he came down the slope.

Ellen turned blindly and ran towards a cluster of large rocks, dodging between them. Abe drew to a halt and calmly dismounted. Now there was nowhere left to run as he approached her, his eyes cold and hard. She flattened herself against a boulder and it was then that she noticed the whip in his hand.

'You just caused a heap o' trouble, lady. I guess I'm gonna have to teach you a lesson so you won't try to run away no more.'

Ellen screamed as the whip sang through the air, jumping aside so that it struck the rock. She fumbled for the fish-handled knife and drew it out again but Hank's next blow knocked it from her hand. She dived for it while dodging the whip once more, then threw a fistful of sand into her tormentor's eyes. He staggered back with an oath, then, finding the knife,

Ellen lunged at him at him in desperation. His eyes streaming, Hank leaped aside as the blade tore along his ribs and struck her hard across the face so that she fell to the ground. Before she could stumble to her feet, however, he drew out his pistol.

'I've had enough trouble from you, bitch!' he shouted as he thumbed back the hammer.

'Drop it, Hank!'

Ellen's tormentor spun around to face Abe who was pointing a rifle at him.

'I'm through takin' orders from you. This girl's nothin' but trouble, so I'm gonna get rid of her and then we'll deal with Casey my way.'

Abe shook his head. 'Jack Hartigan put me in charge of this outfit so you'll do like I tell you. Now put that gun away.'

Hank curled his lip in contempt. 'There ain't much of an outfit left, except you and me. I reckon Jack will be none too pleased when he hears about the mess you've made of things and probably thank me for takin' charge.'

'I won't ask you again, Hank. Put that gun back in its holster.'

There was a pause as the two men stood weighing each other up, each armed and ready to fire.

'There ain't no sense in us fightin' each other,' said Hank. 'It'll take both of us to fix Casey.'

Abe appeared to hesitate, but then nodded as he lowered the rifle. 'I figure you're right about that.'

Hank grinned, then his body swung round in an arc. Ellen screamed as the pistol was aimed at her once more and shut her eyes as a shot rang out. When she opened them again, Hank was lying in a crumpled heap at her feet, a gaping wound in his back.

'You can ride his horse, yours broke a leg,' Abe said, gesturing with the rifle.

'You saved my life just then, Mr Morgan. Why don't you let me go now?'

Abe shook his head. 'I can't do that. As long as you're my hostage, I still got the upper hand over Casey. Come on, let's move.'

Ellen obeyed reluctantly and Abe ensured that she was bound more securely this time. She flinched and turned away as he shot her lame horse, then the two of them set off once more towards Paradise.

★ ★ ★

By the time Jimmy and Tom arrived at the scene the buzzards were tucking into what was left of Hank and the horse. Tom examined the sets of tracks carefully.

'It looks like the girl tried to escape. She fell from the horse or it was shot down coming down that bank. Then she was recaptured. But why was he shot, I wonder?'

Jimmy pointed to the revolver lying near Hank's body. 'He was probably about to shoot Ellen. I'd say Abe killed him because he wants to keep her alive, but the question is, for how long?'

'Until he's taken care of you, I guess. There are two of us against him, Jimmy, so why don't we attack?'

'It's too dangerous. He might shoot Ellen or try to use her as a shield. No, we have to wait and be patient.'

'I don't get it. What's he planning? Once he reaches the town she's bound to call for help, and the sheriff won't let him parade a kidnapped woman through the street.'

Jimmy swung himself back into the saddle. 'I've been thinking the same thing myself. Still, I guess we'll find out what his plans are soon enough.'

Suddenly, Tom pointed to a figure approaching them from the east. It was an Apache mounted on a white horse and as the man drew closer, Jimmy recognized him as Running Bear. Tom exchanged greetings with him and the two men held an animated conversation, which he then translated for Jimmy.

'He's come to warn us that another band of young Apaches have broken out of the reservation and gone on the warpath. They are on the lookout for wagon trains and small groups of travellers, but as long as we are with him we'll be safe. I've told him about Abe and Miss Garrett and he says we must catch them up as soon as possible so that his presence can protect her from harm from the Apaches.'

'I'm grateful to you, Running Bear, but we must be careful when we approach Morgan. He is likely to shoot at us and may harm the girl.'

The old man nodded to show that he had understood, and then led the way ahead of them, setting a brisk pace. Within an hour Abe and Ellen came within sight and Tom suggested riding up to them showing a white cloth as a flag of truce. Jimmy had a spare shirt in his saddle-bag which they tied to the end of Running Bear's spear.

'It's best if I go. He's more likely to shoot if he sees either you or an Apache but he doesn't know me,' suggested Tom. Jimmy agreed reluctantly and watched his friend gallop away, waiting anxiously to see what would happen.

Abe drew to a halt and turned as Tom rode towards him. He drew out his rifle and took aim as horse and rider got nearer.

'Can't you see he's carrying a white flag? Don't shoot, Mr Morgan,' pleaded Ellen.

'It could be a trick,' muttered Abe. 'OK, mister, that's close enough,' he called out as Tom came within fifty yards of them. 'What do you want?'

'There are Apaches in this area and they'll attack if they see you. My friend Running Bear is just behind me and you'll be left alone if you're with him.'

Abe looked up and saw the old Apache approach, his hand raised in a gesture of peace, with Casey beside him. He fired a warning shot on the ground and Tom's horse reared in fright so that he had to fight to control it.

'That was a warnin' and it's the last

one you'll get from me. Any friend of Casey's, especially if he's an Apache or a half-breed, ain't no friend of mine. Now stay back, all of you or the girl will be the first one to get a bullet!'

'Wait just a minute, Morgan,' called Jimmy, riding to the front of the small group. 'Let's settle this now, just the two of us. You can draw first and, whoever wins, everyone else just walks away.'

Abe shook his head. 'No, Casey. I ain't about to wind up in the ground like poor Billy. I'm takin' your girl to Jack Hartigan's ranch. You come there unarmed to answer for what you've done and then I'll let her go.'

'You're a fool, Morgan. You don't stand a chance against the Apaches and besides, Sheriff Hopper won't let you take her through Paradise as your prisoner.'

Abe chuckled as he lowered his rifle. 'You don't expect me to believe that Apache story, do you? Anyhow, I can bypass the town to get where I'm goin' and if you ain't there by sundown tomorrow the girl dies.' Then he turned his rifle away from them and pointed it at Ellen. 'Now, wait here until we're out of sight or you know what will happen.'

They watched helplessly as Abe led his captive away, Ellen turning her head to stare pleadingly at Jimmy as she grew smaller against the horizon. He swallowed hard, desperately hoping that they got to the ranch before the Apaches spotted them.

'What do we do now?' asked Tom.

'We'll wait until they're out of sight and then follow their trail to Paradise. That's our only option.'

★　★　★

The tension was almost unbearable as they watched Abe and Ellen vanish into the desert. Then Running Bear took the lead and they set off once more. They remained alert for any sound but there was only an eerie silence, broken by the occasional breeze. After an hour's ride, however, the smell of flesh decaying in the hot sun greeted their nostrils and they headed towards it. The source of the smell was a cavalry troop, all killed by Apaches judging by the expertise with which they had been scalped. Jimmy waved angrily at the buzzards that settled on the corpses and they flew off briefly.

'That won't do any good and we haven't time to bury them,' Tom reminded him gently.

'I know. The poor devils must have been sent out to round up those renegade Apaches but were attacked themselves. There's Lieutenant Ross over there.' He pointed to the young officer's body, pierced by three arrows, a revolver still clutched in his dead hand. Jimmy did not want to look but was somehow transfixed by the dead man's gaze and remained so until Tom pulled him away. As he followed Running Bear back to the trail, the images of the horror he had witnessed seemed to have burned themselves into his brain and remained there for some time afterwards.

* * *

Just over an hour earlier Ellen had screamed in horror upon witnessing the same scene. Abe spun around and clapped a hand over her mouth. 'Don't make a sound, damn it. If there are any Apaches still around they'll be down on us,' he hissed.

'Jimmy was telling the truth,' she said tremblingly when Abe eventually released her. 'We should go back and look for the others. We'll be safe with that old Indian.'

Abe quickly scanned the surrounding landscape. 'I don't see any sign of them Apaches now. Maybe they've moved on.'

'You can't be sure of that, though, can you?'

Abe shrugged. 'You can't be sure of anything in this world, except dyin' sometime. We got just as much chance if we keep on where we're goin' as we would if we turned back. Apaches are crafty devils, there's no tellin' what they'll do.'

He turned back to Ellen then and saw that her features had frozen in a mask of fear. With one hand she pointed ahead of them to the ridge of a canyon that his eyes had looked upon just moments earlier. There, lined up along it, he now saw a score of Apaches. Abe looked desperately about him and spotted a cluster of rocks and boulders less than a hundred yards away. He cut the rope that bound her horse to his, shouted at Ellen to follow him as fast as she could, and then headed towards them. She immediately galloped after him, the instinct for self-preservation overcoming her fear.

The Apaches let out a war cry and tore down the canyon in pursuit, but they were far enough away to allow Abe and Ellen to reach the shelter of the rocks. Abe checked his rifle and quickly cut the rope binding her wrists before tossing Ellen a revolver.

'I sure hope you can shoot.'

'I hope so too; I haven't had that much practice,' she told him.

5

They crouched behind the rocks, waiting for the Apaches to come within range. Ellen gripped her revolver tightly, trying desperately to control her fear. They were outnumbered ten to one and the Apaches were superb fighters. What chance could they possibly have?

'They'll have got themselves all fired up, maybe had some whiskey by now after killin' them soldiers earlier,' Abe told her, as if reading her thoughts. 'They probably think we're easy meat, so they might make a few mistakes.'

Moments later they were both firing as the enemy bore down on them. Abe showed himself to be a good shot, killing five warriors in quick succession while Ellen did better than she expected. Her first shot missed but her second sent an Apache tumbling from his horse. A third shot hit one of them in the shoulder and he bent over in pain as Abe finished him off. She then hit another rider full in the face but by now the enemy was much closer and a painted warrior in a red shirt leaped at her from his horse. She fired again as his body loomed over hers and he fell dead to the ground.

The Apaches now tried to encircle them. Ellen swung around, firing blindly as one of them rode at her from behind. The bullet struck his horse and he jumped from the animal as it fell. Abe then turned and shot him in the chest as he ran at them. The others now suddenly began to fall back and retreated back to the canyon.

'They're running away!' shouted Ellen excitedly.

'Well, we killed half of 'em, so I guess they figure the two of us ain't worth it. Besides, they don't need to finish us off.'

'Why not?'

Abe pointed to where their horses

had been tethered. 'Look, the ones who attacked from behind were just to keep us occupied while our horses were stolen. Everything was in the saddle-bags, so they meant to leave us on foot with no food or water.'

'Then we'll just have to wait for Jimmy and his friends to catch us up.'

Abe grinned at her in response. 'You'd like that, wouldn't you?' Then he turned his attention to the horse Ellen had wounded. He removed a knife from his belt and leaned on the animal as he expertly extracted the bullet from the hole. Then, taking a small flask from inside his jacket, he poured some whiskey over the wound to cleanse it. After a few minutes, the horse staggered to its feet and Abe triumphantly held up the buffalo-skin container full of water that the previous owner had kept slung around the animal's neck.

Ellen pointed the revolver at him and pulled back the hammer. 'I'm not going anywhere with you,' she said calmly.

'Is that a fact? Well, lady, if you'd

counted the bullets you'd have figured that there's none left.'

Ellen squeezed the trigger as he walked towards her and Abe smiled again as he heard the sound of an empty chamber. He took the gun from her and hauled her to her feet.

'You get on this horse behind me and don't cause any trouble,' he warned her. She obeyed with an obvious show of reluctance and they headed off into the desert once more. It was obvious that their progress would be considerably slowed down and the others were bound to catch them up, yet Abe appeared unconcerned. Ellen could not help thinking that he had already taken this into consideration and shuddered inwardly as she wondered what his plans might be.

★ ★ ★

When Jimmy and his companions reached the cluster of rocks, Tom studied the ground closely. He pointed to a set of tracks leading away from them and remarked upon how deep they were.

'Two people riding one horse, do you think?' Jimmy asked him.

Tom nodded. 'I'd say so. They must have sheltered behind those rocks and managed to fight them off.'

'Where are they now, I wonder?' Jimmy peered through his spyglass. 'They can't have got far but I see no sign of them.'

They continued to follow the trail, while up in the canyon above them Abe took aim with his rifle. Ellen lay bound and gagged beside him but she was determined not to remain a helpless spectator in the drama that was about to unfold. The three travellers moved closer, reaching a point where the tracks stopped abruptly. Abe had carefully covered the next set leading to the canyon with sagebrush. The three men paused: Jimmy was in front, the old Apache next to him. Slowly, he squeezed the trigger.

Ellen was lying on her side, watching her captor closely. As soon as his finger began to move she lashed out with her bound feet, kicking him sharply in the shoulder. Abe swore as he was knocked off balance and the gun lurched sideways when fired. Running Bear was hit squarely in the chest and Jimmy turned to see him tumble from his horse as the shot echoed around the surrounding walls of rock. The two survivors then headed for the foot of the canyon, where they could not be seen easily from above. Abe fired twice more while they were on the move but he had missed his chance.

'Your tricks won't save him,' Abe told Ellen roughly as he cut the rope binding her ankles and hauled her to her feet. He pushed her in front of him as he scurried along the path to the cave where their horse was tethered. Having studied the terrain, Abe knew that the path divided beyond the cave and that in one direction it ran down the opposite side. By following it, he could emerge behind his opponents. Raising the rifle slightly, he administered a sharp blow to the back of Ellen's head, then caught her as she fell. Knowing what she was capable of, it was wise not to take any chances. Then Abe slung her unconscious body over the horse's back and set off down the path.

'It's no use, Morgan, give it up!' shouted Jimmy. 'You've got one horse and two men after you. Let Ellen go and we'll call it quits!'

'I'm in no mood to quit, Casey,' said a voice behind them.

They both turned and saw Abe standing behind them, the muzzle of his rifle placed against the unconscious Ellen's head. 'Let me see you get down and move away from those horses,' he told them. They dismounted slowly and Abe moved a step closer, keeping pace with the horse but without moving his gun one inch. He gestured for them to untie their gun belts and they obeyed, dropping their weapons to the floor.

Abe did not take his eyes off them as he moved the revolvers aside with his boot.

At that moment Abe spotted a scorpion just in front of his horse. The animal snorted and stepped back as the creature approached and Abe quickly crushed it with his boot, moving the rifle away from Ellen as he did so. In a flash Jimmy dived to the ground and retrieved his gun. He fired as Abe swung the rifle towards him, knocking the weapon from his adversary's hands. By this time, Tom had also picked up his gun and both men now had Abe covered.

'Why didn't you just kill me when you had the chance?'

Jimmy shook his head. 'Killing you won't solve anything. Hartigan will just send more men after me. Now, you ride back to that ranch of his and tell him I'll wait for him in Paradise. If he wants to put an end to me, that's where I'll be.'

Tom gently lifted Ellen down from the horse and Abe got on it before issuing a grim warning. 'You're both crazy. Paradise is Jack Hartigan's town and he'll have you in a box by sundown tomorrow.' Then he rode off ahead of them.

Jimmy laid Ellen gently on the ground, using a rolled up blanket as a pillow, then he helped Tom to bury Running Bear. By the time they had finished she was beginning to stir and he gave her some water from his canteen as she opened her eyes to smile at him before wincing at the pain in her head.

'What happened? The last thing I remember was that dreadful man, Morgan holding a gun on me after he tried to shoot you.'

'He tried being too clever and we got you back.'

'Did you shoot him?'

'No. I sent him back to his boss with a message to meet me in Paradise.'

Ellen sat up sharply, then frowned as pain shot through her. 'We've got to get back to Tucson where it's safe.'

Jimmy shook his head. 'There isn't anywhere safe from Jack Hartigan. I've got to go back and finish this where it all started. Then we can begin a new life together.'

'There won't be any new life if you get yourself killed.' She turned to Tom. 'You're the man with the white flag, aren't you? If you're his friend, please try to talk some sense into him before it's too late.'

'Jimmy knows what he's doing. It won't be much of a life if you have to keep looking over your shoulder all the time. Besides, think how many people have died already because of Jack Hartigan's lust for revenge. Someone has to put a stop to it.'

Slowly, she forced herself upright. 'Well, I guess if I can't stop you, I'd better come with you to Paradise.'

'It might be safer for you to go back to Tucson and wait for me there.'

'You mean travel alone through the desert when there are still Apaches on the warpath? Do you want me to finish up as a squaw?'

'She's right. The lady would be better off with us,' added Tom.

'OK, I guess you're coming with us,' conceded Jimmy, 'but stay close if you want to avoid trouble.'

'I'll have you know I fought against Apaches today, so I think I can take care of myself pretty well,' said Ellen firmly as she stood up and dusted down her clothes before mounting Running Bear's horse. Then she leaned over and groaned as her head throbbed once more.

'We'll ride slowly until you start to feel better,' said Jimmy as they set off.

★   ★   ★

Ellen's head gradually cleared as the afternoon wore on but their slowed pace and the delays they had already experienced made it impossible for them to reach Paradise that evening. Dusk fell and the cooler air was refreshing. Even so, it had been a long and eventful day for all of them and they felt relieved when they eventually stopped to make camp. They slept late the next morning, rising when the sun was already up to embark upon the last leg of their journey.

Abe Morgan was well ahead of them but both he and his horse were exhausted by the time they arrived at Hartigan's ranch. Jack came outside in his wheelchair to meet him, casting a critical eye over the dusty, travel-worn figure as Abe dismounted.

'Well, did you get him?'

'He's still alive but on his way to town.'

'Where are the others?'

Abe shook his head. 'All dead, boss.'

Jack frowned. 'You'd best come inside and tell me what happened.' Then he spun his chair around without waiting for a reply and headed back towards the house. Abe followed without a word. Once the two men were inside, Jack turned around to face his ramrod.

'Give it to me straight,' he ordered.

'Casey got lucky, hooked up with some half-breed and a bunch of Apaches. Half the men got killed that way. When we were at Fort Bowie I got hold of this woman who happened to be his girl. We took her with us to make him follow but Casey's smart. He and that half-breed picked us off, even got the girl back too.' Abe thought it best to leave out details of how he had ended up killing two of the men himself.

Jack wheeled himself over to a cabinet and poured out a generous measure of whiskey, which he then downed in one swallow. 'I sent you out with ten hand-picked men and all you've got to show for it are excuses.'

'It weren't nobody's fault, boss. Casey just ran into some good luck and, like I said, he's very smart.'

Jack snorted. 'I wonder, Abe. Is he smart or are you just dumb?'

Now it was Abe's turn to get angry. 'Twenty years I've worked for you and I treated Billy like he was my own. Do you think you're the only one who wants Casey dead? I rode days through the desert, fought Apaches and watched good friends die, so if that's all you've got to say to me I might as well quit.'

Abe turned and headed for the door but Jack called him back. 'Wait! I guess I was a little too hard on you then. I'm sorry.'

It was the first time Abe had heard Jack Hartigan apologize for anything in all the years he had known him. He stopped with his hand on the door handle and slowly turned round. The two men stared at each other for a moment, then Jack held up his glass.

'Come on, sit down and have a drink. Did I hear you say that Casey was headed for Paradise?'

Abe drew up a chair and slumped into it wearily as Jack passed him his whiskey. 'Yeah, that's right. I think he wants to get this thing settled once and for all.'

Jack nodded. 'I guess he got fed up with having you on his trail.'

'What are we gonna do when he gets here?'

'That's what I want to talk to you about,' said Jack as he slowly outlined his plan.

It was late afternoon by the time Jimmy and his companions reached Paradise. Clem Bailey chuckled as he watched them approach the livery stables.

'So, them varmints Jack Hartigan sent out didn't get you after all. I figured you for a man who knows how to take care of himself.'

Jimmy shrugged. 'I guess I was just born lucky.' He introduced Ellen and Tom and the old man took charge of their horses.

'Abe Morgan rode through here a few hours since. He was all alone and looked none too pleased,' Clem told them.

'With all ten of his men dead and me still alive, it's no wonder.'

'What did you come back for, anyhow? You'll only find trouble here.'

'Isn't there any law in this town, Mr Bailey?' asked Ellen, indignantly.

Clem nodded. 'We got a sheriff sure enough, but Jack Hartigan's the law. He owns the big ranch, the saloon and most of the land hereabouts. His men spend their money here and he can hire fancy lawyers to make sure he gets his own way.'

'Maybe someone ought to put that to the test,' suggested Tom.

Clem chuckled again. 'A few folks have tried and they're all lyin' in the churchyard. You can go join 'em if you want.'

Jimmy studied the old man for a moment. 'Tell me something. If the sheriff and the people of this town decided to stand up against Jack Hartigan, what would you do?'

Clem sucked on his pipe for a moment. 'A man's gotta stand for somethin' or he ain't much of a man, so I guess I'd do my bit. I don't reckon it'll come to that, though. Folks like to have a quiet life if they can.'

Jimmy answered him with a smile. 'We'll see about that.'

The saloon was almost full when they entered and all eyes turned towards Jimmy as he strode up to the bar. Joe recognized him at once and his eyebrows shot up in alarm.

'You must be crazy, Mr Casey, coming back here like this.'

'Don't worry about me. I wouldn't still be alive if I couldn't take of myself now would I?'

'I guess not.' Joe moved forward and whispered to him in a conspiratorial tone. 'I hear Abe Morgan rode in here alone today. Hartigan's mad as hell that you're still alive. Did you kill all ten of his men?'

'Let's just say I had a little help.' Jimmy tossed some money on the bar. 'Give us three rooms for the night.'

Joe stared at the money. 'I don't want any trouble.'

'We're here to stop trouble, not start it,' Tom told him.

Joe shrugged. 'OK, I just hope you

110

know what you're up against.'

At that moment Sheriff Hopper entered. 'You've some nerve, Casey. What the hell are you doing back here?'

'I was hoping to have a drink, a meal with my friends here, and then a bed for the night. Do you have any objections?'

'Don't get smart with me. I told you once before, I want no trouble in this town.'

'Just who is it who's causing this trouble?' demanded Ellen angrily. 'Jack Hartigan sent ten men out after Jimmy to hunt him down like a dog. Those same men kidnapped and threatened me. A sheriff is supposed to protect the innocent, not help the guilty.'

Hopper shifted uneasily. 'I'm sorry about what happened to you, but my responsibility is for what goes on in this town, not outside it.'

'Then by my reckoning, Sheriff, it's your job to protect everyone in this town from harm. Am I right?' Jimmy asked him.

Hopper nodded slowly. 'What's your point, Casey?'

Jimmy turned and addressed the crowd assembled in the saloon. 'My point is this. I'm here in this town and I need protection from Jack Hartigan, who keeps trying to kill me. Now, maybe you think that what happens to an outsider doesn't matter, but Hartigan might decide he wants to kill any one of you. Is the law going to protect you or is your sheriff going to tell you to just go and die somewhere else in order to keep the peace?'

A murmur ran through the crowd and Jimmy turned back to the sheriff. 'I made life easy for you a few days ago by riding out of here, but this time I'm not leaving. So what are you going to do about it?'

'I could lock you up in the jail for your own protection, I guess.'

'What will you do when Hartigan sends men to break the door down, drag Jimmy out and lynch him?' asked Tom.

'That's a fair point, but you're putting the people of this town in danger by staying here. Can't you see that?'

'I think that it's Jack Hartigan who's doing that,' said Ellen.

At that moment, a bespectacled figure in a dark suit stepped forward and coughed nervously to clear his throat. Jimmy recognized him as Seymour, the bank clerk who had been present at the fateful card game when Billy Hartigan met his end.

'For what it's worth, I happen to think that both Mr Casey and Miss Garrett are right. I don't consider myself to be a brave man and I abhor violence, but it seems to me that a town worthy of the name Paradise ought to be able to offer a place of safety, a refuge to those in danger.'

'Those are very fine sentiments, Mr Seymour, but don't you realize the risk we'd all be taking?' Hopper asked him.

Seymour nodded gravely. 'Indeed I

do, Sheriff, but I say that it is imperative we take that risk. All of us have a duty to uphold the law and the right of any visitor to our town to remain here unmolested, even when our own lives are at stake. If we fail in that duty, what future does our town have? We will all have surrendered to the law of the gun!'

A murmur of assent ran through the crowd and Jimmy sensed that the mood had swung in his favour.

'What do you say to that, Sheriff?'

Hopper seemed to struggle with a conflicting set of impulses for a moment before he made up his mind. 'All right, if you're set on staying here, I guess I've a duty to help. Right now, I need some volunteers to swear in as deputies. Who's with me?'

Half a dozen hands shot up and the sheriff nodded with satisfaction. 'Good. Now, go home and get your rifles. Then meet me back here in ten minutes.'

'Clem Bailey said he'd be willing to do his part if the people of Paradise decided to stand up for themselves,' Jimmy added.

Hopper laughed mirthlessly. 'I bet he thought the day would never come in his lifetime. Very well, I'll go fetch him.'

As the sheriff headed towards the door, Jimmy called after him. 'Thanks for what you're doing. I know it's not easy.'

The older man paused for a moment. 'Well, it's not just one man we're defending but the law itself and nobody's above the law. That's something I forgot lately.'

Back at his ranch, Jack Hartigan had assembled every man he could spare. Each one was armed, mounted and carried a blazing torch. Hartigan himself had been lifted up on to a wagon and Abe Morgan sat beside him holding the reins, while two men rode shotgun in the back. The boss looked at each man in turn before he began to address them.

'Now, you all know what we're gonna have to do if Casey don't come out or the sheriff refuses to hand him over. If any man hasn't got the stomach for it he can get paid off and leave right now.' There was a brief silence while he waited to see if anyone would speak up but no one did. Hartigan allowed himself a grunt of satisfaction, then gave the order to ride into town.

The streets of Paradise were eerily silent that afternoon. The livery, saloon and grocery store remained closed as the inhabitants locked themselves inside their homes. Almost every window was covered by shutters, as if a sandstorm was expected at any moment. Sheriff Hopper had managed to persuade an additional four men, including Clem Bailey, to serve as deputies, so there were now ten of them spread out along the rooftops of the main street, each armed with a rifle. Hopper stood alone in the centre of town, waiting for Hartigan's arrival in the hope that he could talk some sense into the man. Meanwhile, Jimmy waited in an upstairs room of the hotel with Tom and Ellen.

At last the thunder of hoofs sounded in the distance and gradually drew closer. The three of them watched as more than twenty armed riders bearing blazing torches rode along the main street behind a wagon driven by Abe Morgan. Jimmy guessed that the man beside him was Jack Hartigan.

'They're going to burn us out!' screamed Ellen in terror.

'Take it easy,' Jimmy urged her. 'There's no sense in starting to panic.'

'But what are we going to do? They'll kill us all!'

'For now, I suggest that we just stay calm and wait to see what happens.'

The riders all drew to a halt as Hopper stepped forward to meet them, but it was Hartigan who spoke first.

'I want Casey out here now or my men will burn this town to the ground.'

Hopper shook his head. 'As long as I'm sheriff of this town, no man will be turned over to a lynch mob. Now I'm telling you to turn your men around and go back home. This revenge of yours has gone far enough.'

Hartigan did not take his eyes off the sheriff as he gave his orders. 'OK boys, spread yourselves out and get ready to start some fires!'

'Goddamn you!' shouted Hopper as he went for his gun, but Abe drew first and shot him dead. As the sheriff fell, the men on the rooftops began firing at the members of Hartigan's gang and several of them tumbled to the ground. The rest soon abandoned their attempts to set the town ablaze and took cover to return fire. However, nearly half of the torches were thrown and some of the buildings along the main street quickly burst into flame.

Jimmy shattered the glass window of the hotel room with the barrel of his rifle and took aim at the men riding shotgun on Hartigan's wagon. He squeezed the trigger and watched as first one and then the other fell back dead. He had Hartigan in his sights but

Abe Morgan wisely drove the wagon further down the street. Jimmy cursed loudly and handed his rifle to Tom.

'Take up my place here, I'm going after those two.'

Ellen seized his arm. 'Don't, Jimmy! They'll kill you.'

'They'll kill me sooner or later anyway if I don't get to them first.' Then he pulled away from her and was gone.

6

The scene which greeted him outside was like a battlefield. Bullets flew in all directions while clouds of smoke and the smell of burning filled the air. Townspeople dodged the crossfire and falling splinters as they stumbled from their blackened homes. All around lay the bodies of Hartigan's men and those deputies who had been hit and had fallen from the rooftops. Among them, Jimmy recognized Seymour, the bespectacled bank clerk, who had spoken so eloquently in defence of the law and had now paid for it with his life. He dodged quickly between the buildings and then came upon two of Hartigan's men. They had their backs to him and swung around at his approach. Jimmy shot one of them through the heart but wounded the other man in the arm. The man's rifle fell immediately from numbed fingers.

'Where's your boss?'

The man hesitated as he cowered against the building which had provided his hiding place, and pointed down the street. 'There's a corner just up ahead. I saw the wagon turn down it.'

Jimmy hauled the man to his feet and shoved him ahead. 'Lead the way. If you try to give any warnings I'll shoot.'

Meanwhile, Ellen had watched from the hotel window as Jimmy disappeared into the chaos below. She called after him to come back.

'Let him go. If he gets Hartigan it will all be over,' Tom told her as he took another shot with his rifle.

Tears streamed down her face as she protested in reply: 'He's going to get killed out there, I just know he will.' Then, before he could stop her, Ellen fled from the room, ran down the stairs and out into the street after Jimmy.

★　★　★

By this time Jimmy and his prisoner had reached the corner without further mishap. Jimmy peered around it, his gun in the other man's ribs. He saw the wagon ahead and the two men arguing about what they should do next.

'I say we move out back to the ranch. Our boys are gettin' slaughtered out there,' Abe was saying.

'They've lost men too, and there's been a lot of damage. We should press ahead until they give up,' replied Hartigan.

Jimmy turned to his prisoner. 'I want you to shout a warning that Jimmy Casey's further up this street. Just remember there's a gun at your back.' Then he ducked into a doorway as he shoved the man forward.

At that moment there was a shout from behind and he turned to see Ellen running up the street towards him, calling his name. His prisoner took advantage of Jimmy's moment of distraction to make a run for it. He cannoned into Ellen as she approached, knocking her to the ground. Jimmy ran up and helped her to her feet as the man ran off. Before they had no time to speak, however, Abe Morgan burst round the corner, driving his wagon at high speed. Hartigan was beside him, firing his rifle as they passed: splinters flew from the building behind them as the shots narrowly missed. Jimmy cursed as the vehicle tore off down the street; he fired after it. Then he heard Ellen scream. He turned, but a horse being ridden hard by one of Hartigan's men knocked him sideways. The thunder of hoofs was the last thing he heard before everything dissolved into a black void.

It was several hours before he awoke. His head throbbed as he raised it from the pillow. He grimaced with pain as he tried to sit up and Tom gently pushed him back down onto the bed.

'Take it easy for a while, Jimmy. Dr Maddox says you haven't broken any bones but your bruises will hurt for some time yet.'

'Where's Ellen?' he demanded, remembering the scream he had heard.

Tom hesitated before giving his reply. 'The rider who knocked you down grabbed her. We think Hartigan's got her over at his ranch.'

Jimmy fought down a rapidly rising tide of panic. 'I can't just lie here like this. I've got to do something.'

At that moment Clem Bailey emerged from the shadows. The old man shook his head as he removed his pipe from his mouth. 'Just now you ain't in no fit state to go nowhere. That pretty young woman o' yours won't come to no harm while Hartigan needs her as his hostage, anyhow.'

'Clem's right. Let's wait until we see what his next move's going to be,' added Tom.

Jimmy shook his head. 'Who's in charge around here now? I saw Hopper get shot, so somebody must be acting as sheriff.'

Clem sighed in response. 'The fact is this town took quite a beatin' from

Hartigan's men. Some houses and the grocery store got burned down, six men got killed and two more injured, besides you. There's not much stomach for another fight and nobody's willin' to take charge, except Tom here.'

Only then did Jimmy notice the door to his room. It was made up of iron bars. 'What the hell am I doing in jail? What's wrong with Tom acting as sheriff, anyway?' he demanded.

Tom and Clem exchanged looks and the two men shifted uncomfortably. 'We figured this would be the safest place, seein' as some folks favour just handin' you over to Hartigan,' Clem told him. 'As for Tom, the idea of a half-breed sheriff didn't go down too well with most people.'

Jimmy clenched his fists and attempted to sit up once more, eventually managing to do so. 'What the hell's wrong with these people? Do they want Hartigan stamping all over them for the rest of their lives?'

'Take it easy, son. They're just scared,

that's all,' Clem told him. 'I figure we need some help from outside.'

'What about the cavalry? After all, the south west is still under military jurisdiction,' said Tom. 'I could ride out there on Banjo and be back within four days.'

Jimmy nodded thoughtfully. 'That's a good suggestion, but how do we stall Hartigan in the meantime?'

'I guess we could pretend that you're so badly injured you can't be moved at the moment and might even die,' said Tom.

'Yeah, Hartigan's gonna want to be the one who ends your life and for you to know he's takin' his revenge. I reckon he'll be prepared to wait a few days for that privilege,' added Clem. 'You two wait up while I go get Doc Maddox back here. He'll need to be in on it.'

The old man returned a few minutes later with the doctor. Maddox was an imposing figure in a neatly pressed dark suit which matched his iron-grey hair and trim beard. He peered at his patient over a pair of half-moon spectacles, then removed a roll of bandages from his bag. He gently wrapped Jimmy's head and much of his face with one long strip and then asked him to lift his shirt so that he could wind another one around his chest. Lastly, a sling was added, in to which Jimmy placed his right arm.

'There now, if anyone comes to look at you, just pretend to be asleep,' said Maddox as he surveyed his handiwork. He snapped his bag shut and stood up straight. 'I think the best thing now would be for me to ride over to Hartigan's ranch and tell him that you're very badly injured and barely conscious. I'll suggest that you be handed over when you're fit enough to be moved and that this won't be for some days yet.'

'Thanks, Doc. Let's hope he buys it,' Jimmy told him.

Maddox shrugged. 'I'll do my best. If I get a moment to speak to that young lady of yours I'll try to reassure her.' Then he turned and went outside where some townspeople gathered around him. 'Mr Casey is far too ill to be moved,' he told them. 'The best thing you folks can do is to bury the dead and get on with clearing up the mess the town's been left in.'

'That won't do us no good!' protested Ben Fleming, a short, stocky and pugnacious individual who owned the gunsmith's shop. 'Hartigan and his men will be back soon enough and this time there won't be nothin' left to rebuild.'

There were shouts of agreement from among the crowd and calls from some for Jimmy to be handed over straight away. Maddox raised his hands to quieten them and fixed the gunsmith with a hard stare.

'I reckon you ought to simmer down a little, Mr Fleming — '

'Don't tell me to simmer down, damn it!' yelled the gunsmith. 'My shop has been burned to the ground and I ain't about to lose my home too on account of some drifter who's brought this town nothin' but trouble.'

'Most folks here have lost property, some have been injured and others lost their lives because they wanted to defend Paradise and the rule of law,' replied Maddox. 'It seems we've lost that battle, so I'm going over to see Hartigan now. I'll tell him that Mr Casey will be handed over to him once he's fit to be moved in exchange for the safety of our town and the life of the young lady he's holding hostage.'

'I still don't see why Casey can't be handed over now,' insisted Fleming, his tone still belligerent.

'Hartigan's mad at the people of this town for trying to fight him; I don't think a dead body will be enough to satisfy his lust for revenge. That's all he'll get if we hand Mr Casey over to him now. I suggest we let our prisoner recover and then Hartigan can take out his anger on him.'

There was a moment's silence while

the townspeople digested this information. Then a reluctant murmur of assent went up and the crowd parted so that Maddox was able to push his way through. Fleming said nothing further but scowled at the doctor's retreating back.

'I'm glad he didn't tell them about the cavalry,' said Tom after watching this altercation through the window. 'We can't be sure that Hartigan won't get to hear about it once other people know what we've planned.'

Jimmy shook hands with his friend as Tom made ready to leave. 'Good luck, and ride carefully. We're depending on you.'

'Don't worry. I'll be back with those horse soldiers before you know it.'

Back at Hartigan's ranch the table had been laid for dinner. Jack Hartigan sat at the head of the table with Abe beside him. A place was left empty where Billy had once sat. Ellen sat sullenly at the opposite end of the table, her food untouched. She watched with evident distaste as Hartigan dipped a hunk of bread into a bowl of stew and shovelled it into his mouth. He looked up and met her gaze unflinchingly.

'Tuck in, Miss Garrett. I like to see that my guests eat well.'

'I'm no guest, Mr Hartigan. I'm a prisoner,' she replied coldly.

'I was being polite but even prisoners have to eat, don't they?'

'If you're so polite, why do you speak with your mouth full?'

Hartigan chuckled. 'I like a woman who speaks her mind. You can stay on here if you want, once we've dealt with Casey. It's a long time since we've had anyone as pretty as you around the place.'

Ellen ignored him and turned to the maid who was pouring her some coffee. 'Will you show me to the room where I'm supposed to sleep, please?'

Hartigan's face darkened. 'I give the orders in this house and you'll sit there until I tell you otherwise. Speak your mind if you want but don't forget who's in charge.'

'Oh I won't forget anything about you, Mr Hartigan. If Jimmy comes to any harm on your account, I'll do everything in my power to see that justice is done.'

Hartigan wiped his mouth with his napkin. 'Justice is exactly what Jimmy Casey is going to get. It might not be according to the law, but it'll be justice all right.'

Their conversation was interrupted by the sound of galloping hoofs and Hartigan turned to Abe Morgan. 'Go see who that is,' he told him.

Abe went to the window and looked out. 'It's Doc Maddox. What does he want?'

A moment later there was a knock at the door. Abe opened it, then stepped aside as Maddox removed his hat and asked if he could see Hartigan. The doctor saw Ellen sitting at the table and asked her if she was being treated well.

'She'll come to no harm as long as I

get Casey,' interrupted Hartigan. 'Is that what you've come about?'

Maddox came over to the table and towered over the rancher as Hartigan turned his wheelchair around to face him. 'Mr Casey suffered a severe blow to the head and several other injuries when he was knocked down by that horse.'

'Will he live?'

'He can't be moved at present but, given time, he'll recover sufficiently for you to exact your revenge upon him. He's being cared for in the town jail.'

Hartigan gave a smirk of satisfaction. 'I'm glad you people are starting to see sense. When can I come to collect Casey?'

'He'll be up and about in a week or so.'

Hartigan's eyes narrowed suspiciously. 'What are you trying to pull? I'm not waiting that long.'

Maddox shrugged. 'Mr Casey drifts in and out of consciousness and that could last a few days. I just thought you'd want him fully recovered before you . . . er . . . deal with him.'

'You've got some funny ideas, Doc. If he can stand, ride a horse and feel pain, he'll be ready to take what's comin' to him. Ain't that right, boss?' said Abe.

Hartigan nodded. 'That's right. How long will that take?'

'How about five days?'

'I'll give you four. I'll bring my boys into Paradise at noon on the fourth day and there'd better not be any tricks, understand?'

Maddox nodded. 'Now that's settled, perhaps you'd be kind enough to release Miss Garrett, as a gesture of goodwill.'

Hartigan shook his head. 'No dice, I'm afraid. When Casey wakes up and starts to feel better, he might take it into his head to bust out of that jail. I want him to know that if he gets away from me again, I'll kill the girl.'

Maddox licked his lips nervously. 'I'll be sure to give him that message when he wakes up.'

Hartigan gave a grunt of satisfaction. 'You do that. We'll have Miss Garrett with us when we come into town, so it will be a straight swap: her freedom for his life. Now go on, get out of here.'

Maddox looked over at Ellen and gave her a nod as he turned to go. She rose from her chair and grabbed his arm. 'Tell him I'm all right, that I love him and not to worry about me.' The doctor patted her hand reassuringly, then left.

Hartigan turned back to face Ellen. 'Well, the townspeople's little rebellion didn't last long, after all. Folks always do what's best for themselves and their own kin in the end, young lady. That's something you'll learn before you get much older.'

'Not everyone's like you, Mr Hartigan.'

'I'll remind you of that statement when they hand your sweetheart over to me.' He watched as her eyes filled with tears of despair and suddenly he appeared shamefaced. 'You can go on upstairs now if you want,' he added roughly. He turned his chair around as she fled from the room.

When Ellen had gone Abe looked at his boss thoughtfully. 'You could be wrong about those folks. Casey's friends might have somethin' else in mind. What if they're just stallin' for time?'

Hartigan nodded. 'They could be, I guess. You take a ride into town tomorrow and have a peek at Casey. Make sure it's like Maddox said and report back to me.'

'And if it ain't?'

'Then there'll be hell to pay.'

*   *   *

Early the next morning Abe rode into Paradise and tethered his horse outside the jail. He peered in through the window and saw a figure lying on a bed in one of the cells, swathed in bandages. He guessed it was Casey and walked over to the door. Finding it locked, Abe knocked loudly. He heard a shuffling noise and the jangle of keys before it was opened slightly and Clem Bailey's head appeared.

'What do you want, Morgan?'

'I came to check up on Casey. Let me in.'

'He's asleep, now get lost.'

Clem tried to shut the door but the younger man pushed his way in, barged past him and went up to the barred door of the cell. He shouted across to the inert figure but Jimmy did not stir. He called again but Clem interrupted him.

'Can't you see how sick he is? He's gonna be handed over to your boss. Ain't that enough for you?'

Abe looked around suspiciously. 'Where's that half-breed friend of his? I thought he'd be here.'

Clem shrugged. 'I dunno what yer askin' me for. How in hell should I know?'

Abe fixed him with a hard stare. 'You three and the Garrett girl stuck pretty close together as I recall. It's strange, him not bein' here.'

'I ain't seen Tom since yesterday and I already told you I don't know where he is.'

'Don't you think it's odd that he's gone off and left Casey like this?'

'I'm lookin' after Jimmy and I don't need help from anyone else,' replied Clem defiantly.

Abe shook his head. 'Somethin' don't add up here and I'm gonna find out what it is.' Then he turned on his heel and left. Clem watched his retreating back for a moment, then unlocked the cell to talk to Jimmy, who now sat up.

'Did you hear all that?' Clem asked him.

'Yes, I did. Abe will find out that Tom left town and maybe try to follow him, but there's nothing we can do about it.'

'I guess not,' agreed Clem. 'Tom's a smart fella, anyhow, and he's got nearly a day's head start on Morgan. We'll just have to hope Morgan don't catch up.'

'If that happens I'll just have to

surrender to Hartigan. You heard what Maddox said when he came back from the ranch yesterday.'

Clem shook his head. 'It won't come to that,' he said, but with more conviction than he felt. He had known Abe Morgan a long time and the man was nothing if not determined.

Abe was checking the hotel at that very moment and quickly learned that Tom had ridden out of Paradise the previous afternoon on Casey's horse. Wasting no time, he headed quickly back to the ranch to get the fastest horse Hartigan owned, and provisions for several days.

Hartigan was not impressed by Abe's suspicions. 'Look, the man turned out to be a horse thief. What do you expect? He's got Apache blood, hasn't he?'

'Can we afford to take that chance? He might have gone to get help from some place. What about his Apache friends? They'd love to burn this place to the ground and make off with all your stock.'

Hartigan stroked his beard thoughtfully. 'All right, have it your way but turn back if you haven't caught up with Taylor within two days. I want you here for the big showdown.'

Abe nodded his agreement and rode off into the desert. It did not take him long to pick up Tom's trail; he kept up a steady pace as he followed it across the parched landscape. By nightfall he had guessed where his quarry was heading and the realization made him more determined than ever to catch up. There was a full moon and he pressed on through the night, only stopping to rest a few hours before dawn. He was concerned about riding the horse too hard, but that would not matter if he caught up with Tom Taylor in time. Then he could just steal his horse, once he had killed its rider, of course.

7

The sun was up when Tom awoke, but not having an early start did not concern him unduly. With luck, he could still reach Fort Bowie by nightfall and get back to Paradise with the cavalry in time to rescue Jimmy. Besides, it was best not to tire even a fine horse like Banjo too much. At midday he noticed that his mount's ears were twitching and wondered if Banjo sensed that they were being followed. Tom dismounted, put his ear to the ground and felt the vibration from distant hoofs. Someone was riding fast towards him, he knew that much. Recalling that there was a canyon a few miles ahead, he headed swiftly towards it.

Abe had been up at first light, riding hard all the way. The trail was quite fresh now and he knew that he could not be far behind. His horse sweated profusely and snorted with effort as he spurred the hapless animal on to go a little faster. Reluctantly, he stopped for a brief rest and gave the appaloosa some water. Then, after taking a swig from his canteen, he pressed on until he approached a canyon, where the trail ended. Abe slowed to a halt and looked around him, but saw no sign of anyone.

Above him Tom took careful aim with his rifle. At that moment Abe spotted the glint of sunlight on metal. He ducked down in the saddle and moved aside as the shot rang out. The appaloosa whinnied and collapsed beneath him. Abe jumped down as it fell to the ground with a gaping hole in its flanks. Cursing, he drew his revolver and dived behind a boulder for cover.

Tom peered over the ridge but saw only the dead horse. There was no sign of Morgan but he knew that Hartigan's man would soon be climbing up the path towards him. Rather than risk a confrontation, it seemed best to just ride off and leave his adversary stranded. He leaped nimbly up on to Banjo and galloped through the narrow pass and out into the open desert. Abe guessed what was happening and raced across to the appaloosa's carcass where he retrieved his rifle. He ran up the path through the canyon in time to spot the distant figure riding away, took aim and squeezed the trigger. The shot echoed around him and he watched with satisfaction as Tom's body jerked in the saddle. However, he quickly realized that the half-breed was only wounded and was continuing to ride on. Abe fired once more but his quarry was now out of range. Cursing again, he climbed back down the canyon to collect what provisions he could carry and set off to walk through the desert. With luck the half-breed would bleed to death and the horse would then slow to a halt. If that did not happen, Abe faced a struggle to survive long enough to reach Fort Bowie.

Tom stopped several miles ahead and

staggered over to a large outcrop of rock. He lit a fire with some sagebrush and reluctantly drew out his knife. He was bleeding heavily and the bullet in his shoulder would have to come out. He winced as he poured some whiskey over the wound to clean it, then he inserted the blade to feel for the bullet. Grimacing with pain, he dug it out, then sank to the ground, gasping. Now came the really hard part. Tom was going to have to cauterize the wound if it was not to become infected. He plunged the blade of his knife into the flames and waited a moment. Then, bracing himself, he held it against the torn flesh and allowed it to scorch. A white-hot pain shot through him, racking his whole body; he collapsed, weeping in agony. After a few minutes, he got up on to his knees and used a clean bandanna to make a bandage. When that was done he put his shirt back on, climbed on to Banjo's back and headed for Fort Bowie.

Tom slumped low in the saddle as he

continued his journey. His shoulder throbbed dully and he felt weak from loss of blood, but he hung on grimly. As long as he could ride faster than Morgan could walk, that was all he cared about.

Meanwhile, his pursuer stumbled along some miles behind, the distance between them gradually widening. As the afternoon wore on, Abe's limbs grew heavy so that every step was like carrying a lead weight. He was sorely tempted to discard his rifle but clung on to it stubbornly, knowing that he would need it should he manage to catch up with Tom. His mouth was drier than a rattlesnake's cave but he dare not drink from his canteen again. He would sweat the water out in no time, so it was best to wait until nightfall if he could.

At that moment he heard a rumbling sound in the distance. Abe turned and saw that there was a wagon approaching from behind. He let out a hoarse cry and waved his rifle in the air as the vehicle drew closer to him. The driver brought his team of horses to a halt and studied him carefully. Abe saw that he was a plump, dishevelled individual who wore a sweat-stained shirt and had a battered derby hat pushed to the back of his head. Strands of greying hair poked out from underneath it, and his dark, porcine eyes were set in fleshy features above a scraggy grey beard. The wagon was heavily laden with blankets, clothing and bottles of various kinds so Abe judged him to be a trader.

'You look to be in trouble there, mister,' the stranger said.

'I was on my way to Fort Bowie when some varmint jumped me and stole my horse. I managed to wound him with my rifle but he got away.'

The stranger nodded. 'Well, I'm headed that way myself. You'd best get aboard.'

Abe scrambled up beside his bene-factor and took a grateful swig from the canteen he was offered. 'He'll be on a white horse, a half-breed with a shoulder wound and he's goin' this way.'

The stranger grinned. 'Well, when we catch up he won't be stealin' horses no more, will he?'

★   ★   ★

Back at Hartigan's ranch, Ellen stood on the veranda outside her room and looked down at the horses in the corral below. As always, the place was a hive of activity: there was no chance of being able to climb down and make her escape unnoticed.

'I know what you have in mind, Miss Garrett. You won't get far so just forget it.'

'Don't you ever knock?' she asked as Hartigan wheeled himself into the room.

'A man don't have to knock anywhere in his own home.'

She shrugged. 'I guess not. Besides, jailers don't knock for their prisoners, do they?'

Hartigan drew closer and she shuddered inwardly at his approach. 'Don't be like that, Miss Garrett. The boys enjoy having a pretty woman about the place, just as I do. In fact, I thought we might have a special dinner tonight in your honour.'

'Before you shoot me,' added Ellen sarcastically.

Hartigan shook his head. 'No, it won't come to that. I've promised to exchange you for Casey and I intend to keep my word. I'm grateful, you see. Without you, it would be much more difficult to avenge my boy's death.'

As Hartigan left, she chewed her lip thoughtfully. Doubtless the men would drink more heavily on a special occasion. If she played along for a while it might just provide her with the chance she needed. Ellen leant over the balustrade and peered along the line of buildings until she spotted the stables where the horses were kept overnight. She then left her room and crept downstairs, heading for the front door.

'Just where are you off to?' said a voice behind her.

Startled, she turned abruptly to see Hartigan squatting in his Bath chair in the middle of the hallway. She kept forgetting that the elevator he had installed in the ranch allowed him to move around the house quickly.

'I just wanted to go out for some fresh air. Is that all right?' she asked.

'I guess it can't do any harm.' He paused for a moment, then called out for Burt Paterson, one of his ranch hands, who had been carrying out some repairs inside the house. He appeared almost instantly, his lean muscled frame standing at well over six feet. Ellen recognized him as the rider who had seized her when Hartigan's men attacked Paradise. Paterson's black hair was swept back from his forehead. His dimpled chin and chiselled features made him an attractive figure to the housekeeper and her maids, but Ellen always felt that there was something sinister about his taciturn manner and the catlike way he moved.

'Yeah, boss?' he said enquiringly.

'Miss Garrett would like to go out for a walk around the place. See to it that she doesn't get lost.'

'Sure, I'd be happy to.'

Ellen felt his dark eyes bore into her as he followed her out on to the front porch. She tried to appear nonchalant as she pretended to watch the men about their work and then wandered over to the corral. One of the horses, a chestnut and white pinto, came over and muzzled her cheek. He was clearly friendly and well used to being handled.

'Does this one have a name?' she asked, trying to sound casual.

'He's called Jack. Billy used to ride him,' said Paterson.

She made a mental note to look for Jack when she tried to make her escape. After walking further along she examined the stable door and noticed a heavy padlock. Paterson took out his tobacco pouch and began making a cigarette, but he kept her under his gaze the whole time. She heard the rasp of a match and turned as he started to puff out a cloud of smoke. His eyes met hers through the blue haze.

'You had enough of that fresh air yet?'

Ellen nodded in reply and he followed her back into the house. She had seen enough but could not escape the uneasy feeling that Paterson knew exactly what was on her mind. Despite the warmth of the day, she shivered as she climbed the staircase to her room, aware that he was standing at the bottom watching her as he smoked.

★   ★   ★

Abe felt every jolt of the wagon in his aching limbs, but was wise enough not to complain. The trader, who introduced himself as Woody, kept up a steady pace and there was a good chance of catching up with Tom long before he reached Fort Bowie. Then, in the distance, Abe spotted a lone figure trudging through the desert on a white horse.

'It looks as though that could be the fella you're after,' said Woody, taking a swig from the keg of whiskey he kept stowed in the back.

'It's him all right,' said Abe.

'You can take a shot once we're in range.'

'No, I got somethin' better in mind for him.'

Woody chuckled. 'Yeah, I guess a bullet's too easy for half-breeds who steal honest white men's horses and leave 'em stranded out in this hell-hole.' The wagon picked up speed and quickly gained on Tom, who was not unduly concerned and moved aside to allow the vehicle to pass. He glanced behind as it drew close and reached for his rifle when he recognized Abe. A warning shot was promptly fired over his head and he stuck his hands in the air as the wagon halted beside him.

'I don't know what this man's told you but — '

Woody cut him off. 'Don't give me no lies, you damn half-breed. I know what happened.' The trader aimed a rifle at him while Abe climbed down from the wagon and strode a few feet towards him.

'Get down from that horse,' he said, drawing his revolver.

Tom obeyed reluctantly, realizing that he had no choice. He watched nervously as Abe levelled the gun at him.

'I bet that shoulder wound hurts some, don't it?'

Tom nodded but said nothing.

'Well, I'm gonna put a hole in your other shoulder, one in each knee and maybe one in your gut too. Then we'll see how far you can crawl before you die.'

Tom turned to the trader. 'Are you just going to stand by and let him do this?'

Woody chuckled and took another

swig from his keg of whiskey. 'No, I'm gonna sit and watch. It should prove to be a mighty fine spectacle!'

At that moment a shot rang out and Woody's keg shattered into fragments, causing him to jump up in his seat and look about him wildly. This was followed by the hiss of an arrow flying through the air. It embedded itself in Abe's hand. He dropped his gun immediately and Tom stepped on it. Suddenly, they were surrounded by a group of Apaches, about a dozen in all. Their leader was the young brave, Walks Softly, who had been married to Tom's cousin.

'You have met with trouble, Tom Tames Horses,' said Walks Softly in Apache.

Tom pointed at Abe. 'Yes, from the man who killed Running Bear.'

'Then he is the one we seek,' said Walks Softly.

Abe looked at Tom questioningly. 'What will they do?'

'They will kill you slowly, like you

were going to do to me.'

Abe whipped out a knife with his left hand as the mounted Apaches closed in on him and tried to plunge it into his heart in one swift movement. The warriors anticipated his move, however and seized their intended victim. He glowered at Tom and shouted curses at his assailants as they hustled him away to a torturous death.

Walks Softly pointed at Woody and asked, 'What shall we do with this one?'

The trader was now deathly pale and shaking with fear. He looked pleadingly at Tom. 'I thought you were just a horse-thief who left a man to die in the desert. I figured whatever he wanted to do to you was what you had comin'. Don't let them kill me.'

'Let him go,' said Tom.

'He was about to kill you,' said Walks Softly.

'That was only because of Morgan's lies.'

The other warriors had been investigating the contents of Woody's wagon.

Now one of them approached Walks Softly, holding up a bundle of Apache scalps. Woody swallowed hard and reached for his rifle, but one of the Apaches snatched it away.

'I didn't kill nobody,' he protested. 'I bought 'em from an Indian fighter. Some folks pay good money for that kinda thing.'

'So you bought these scalps from the man who did the killing. Is that right?' asked Tom, staring hard at the trader.

Woody licked his dry lips. 'I guess so. Like I said before, I didn't kill nobody.'

'Perhaps not, but you made money from the deaths of those people. Without men like you, they wouldn't have died in the first place.'

The trader swallowed hard and his porcine features adopted a pleading look. 'Look, maybe we can work this out, cos I got plenty of stuff on the wagon. Why don't you just tell your friends here to take what they want and we can all let bygones be bygones?'

'The lives of Apaches are worth a few

bottles of whiskey and some beads, is that it?'

Woody shrugged nervously. 'I'm just tryin' to get by, that's all.'

'Do you still want to let him live?' Walks Softly asked Tom.

Tom silently picked up the revolver Abe had dropped and aimed it at the trader. Woody screamed as six bullets were fired into his chest; his body twitched as blood spurted from each wound before he slumped sideways and lay still. The warriors then set about burning the wagon, once they had helped themselves to the goods they wanted.

'Now that we have avenged Running Bear, we will cross the white man's border into the land they call Mexico,' announced Walks Softly. Then, bidding Tom farewell, he led his followers away. Tom winced in pain as he climbed into the saddle once more and gently urged Banjo on towards Fort Bowie, which he still hoped to reach by nightfall.

* * *

Back at Hartigan's ranch, a steer had been slaughtered to provide the beef for that evening's dinner. The men bathed and dressed in their Sunday best, a trestle table was set up in the dining room and furniture cleared away to accommodate all the men. Candles were lit and flowers put out. Even Ellen was impressed by all the trouble that had been taken on her behalf, but she was no less determined to escape. If Hartigan thought that she would become more at ease with her situation then he was sadly mistaken. She bided her time however, acting graciously when her presence was toasted and ate the food that was placed in front of her. A fiddler struck up a tune and she took a turn dancing with several of the ranch hands while Hartigan sat clapping his hands in time to the music. He appeared thoroughly pleased with what was going on as she continued to smile sweetly and laugh at the men's jokes.

Ellen was careful to drink as little as possible, but she observed with growing satisfaction that the men were all consuming copious quantities of beer and spirits. At last she rose from the table and made a short speech.

'I'd like to thank Mr Hartigan and all you men for the wonderful evening we've had. It really has been quite delightful. I know that I didn't come here under the best of circumstances and I haven't been an easy guest, but the food and the company this evening has been delightful. Thank you all but I'm afraid I really must bid you goodnight. I'm completely exhausted.'

Hartigan gave her a gracious nod, the men raised their glasses in a final toast and she made her way up the staircase, affecting a weariness she did not feel. Once in her room, Ellen quickly removed the dress that had been provided for the occasion and changed into trousers and a shirt. Then she stepped out on to the veranda and climbed over it, holding on to the balustrade. Then she dropped down, bending her knees to roll over when she hit the ground. Once on her feet again, Ellen made her way to the stables and drew out a hatpin she had found in a drawer in her room. Inserting it carefully in the lock, she twisted it gently until she heard a satisfying click. The door creaked slightly as she opened it and she froze for a moment. Then, once satisfied that no one had heard her, she stepped inside.

The night was cloudless and the moonlight provided shafts of illumination which guided her to Jack's stall. He was sleeping but snorted softly as she stroked his muzzle and whispered to him. Then an oil lamp was turned up and she jumped as light flooded into the stable. She turned and saw that Burt Paterson was standing behind her, holding up the lamp.

'I thought I'd find you here, Miss Garrett. Did you really think I couldn't guess what you were up to this afternoon?' Paterson put the lamp down on a nearby stool and stepped towards her.

'Stay away from me,' she said, backing away from him.

Paterson grinned at her. 'Come on now, don't be like that. If you're real nice to me I won't tell old man Hartigan what you were gonna do. It'll just be our little secret.'

Paterson's hands were gripping her shoulders and his mouth moved hungrily towards hers. The hatpin was still in her hand and she thrust it into him without even thinking about it. His eyes widened as the point entered his heart, his mouth opened but no sound emerged. Burt Paterson was dead. His body knocked against the stool as it fell to the ground and the oil lamp broke as it hit the wooden floor.

Ellen screamed as tongues of flame leaped up around her and the horses reared in terror in their stalls. Seizing the blanket that lay across Jack's back she quickly beat at the spreading fire, but it was beginning to take hold.

Roused by the noise and the smell of smoke, men ran from the house and buckets of water were fetched from the well to douse the flames. The horses were freed and herded into the corral. In the confusion, she looked for another chance to escape and approached one of the horses who had broken away from the others. As she did so, however, powerful arms seized her from behind and two of the men began dragging her back to the house. She kicked out and shouted at them but it was to no avail. As she was bundled through the front door, Ellen saw that Hartigan was there in the hall. He wheeled himself towards her, crimson with rage.

'Damn you, this whole place could have gone up in flames!' he bawled.

'I just wanted to get out of here. Paterson was watching; he followed and tried to rape me. He knocked the lamp over when I fought him off.'

Hartigan looked questioningly at the two men holding her. 'Where's Paterson now?'

'He's dead. We found him with a hatpin stuck in his chest,' one of them replied.

Hartigan stared at her for a moment, his eyes blazing. 'I've half a mind to let each of my men take a turn with you but I'm not a savage, whatever you might think. You'll stay locked up and under guard from now on.' Then he turned once more to her captors. 'Take Miss Garrett upstairs and put her in the other guest room. See to it that she can't leave.'

Ellen's new room was smaller and with no veranda, only a small window that she could not squeeze through. After she was shoved inside a key was turned in the lock and she heard the sound of someone pulling up a chair outside, presumably the guard. Tears of frustration welled up in her eyes and she flung herself, weeping, onto the bed.

8

It was very late when Tom eventually reached Fort Bowie. His wound was no longer bleeding but ached dully and he was weak from loss of blood. He heard the sentry step forward to challenge him.

'I have to speak to your commanding officer right away.'

'Can't it wait until morning?'

Tom shook his head weakly. 'There's a town called Paradise. It's going to be attacked in two days and people will get killed unless the army gets there first.'

The sentry held up a lamp and studied Tom more closely. 'You don't look so good.'

'I've been shot by one of the gang I was telling you about.'

The sentry helped him down from his horse. 'You'd best come with me.'

Tom was in the hospital with a

doctor examining his wound when the commanding officer arrived to speak to him. A tall, thin man with greying hair and side whiskers, he introduced himself as Colonel Steele. He listened intently as the events in Paradise were explained to him, then he gave his decision.

'Well, it's clear to me that there's now gun law in Paradise and we can't have that. At first light I'll send Captain Edward Marcus, one of my most experienced officers, to Paradise with a column of twenty men.'

'That's great news, Colonel. I'll be ready.'

'I'm sure the doctor here will agree with me that you're in no fit state to travel and will only slow the column down,' replied Steele. 'You must remain here and rest for the next few days until your wound has healed.'

'Colonel Steele is right,' the doctor assured him. 'If you want that column to arrive in time, you'd best stay where you are.'

'Will you be taking a supply wagon?' asked Tom

'Yes, of course. We'll need one for food and ammunition,' Steele told him.

'Then I'll ride in that so I don't have to worry about keeping up.'

Steele shook his head. 'That's out of the question. We can't take a sick man on an operation like this.'

Tom raised himself up on to one elbow. 'What if you run into some Apaches? It wouldn't hurt to have someone along who speaks their language, would it?'

'I guess that could save some trouble, sir,' said the doctor.

Steele considered this for a moment. 'Very well, but you travel at your own risk.'

Tom sank back exhausted on to his pillow and drifted into a grateful sleep.

★   ★   ★

Back in Paradise, Jimmy was unable to sleep. He sat up on the narrow bunk and gazed at the moonlight which filtered through the barred window of his cell. Clem and Dr Maddox had dropped by that evening but he had received no other visitors. The townspeople preferred to stay away from the man they planned to hand over to Hartigan, a decision ratified at a council meeting following an almost unanimous vote in favour. Jimmy was sick of the wretched town, its cowardly inhabitants, and of lying around all day swathed in bandages. Had it not been for the need to rescue Ellen, he would already have made his escape. Now all he could do was wait and hope that Tom would arrive back in time.

It was an unusually warm night and the dawn arrived with a dim grey light obscured by clouds and the closeness that heralded a storm. Jimmy groaned when he heard the first roll of thunder and lay anxiously anticipating the deluge as the hours passed. It started before noon and Clem was drenched when he brought him his lunch.

'It doesn't look too good out there,' commented Jimmy. 'If the cavalry get delayed by the weather, Hartigan will have his revenge.'

The old man shook his head. 'He'll have to get past me first,' he declared, waving a pistol in the air in a gesture of defiance.

'No, Clem. There's no point in trying to resist Hartigan's men without outside help. If you really want to do something for me, you can make sure that Ellen gets back to Tucson safely. The army can deal with Hartigan when it arrives here.'

Clem nodded. 'Whatever you say, Jimmy. Let's hope it doesn't come to that.'

Jimmy looked out at the rain. 'Yeah, all we can do right now is hope.'

★   ★   ★

Captain Marcus cursed softly as the teeming columns of rain drenched both men and horses. The land was parched and certainly needed watering, but why did the storm have to happen now? Tom lay in the wagon and listened to the sound of water drumming on the canvas roof. Suddenly the vehicle lurched to one side and some tins fell from the shelf above him, narrowly missing his head.

Marcus poked his head through the flap. 'I'm sorry about that, one of the wheels has got stuck but we'll have it out soon.'

'How much time have we lost?'

Marcus mopped his wet face with a handkerchief. 'Let's not worry about that yet. Provided the storm doesn't last more than a few hours, we should reach Paradise before Mr Casey's time is up.' The officer was a practical man and not one given to panic. His craggy features with dark eyes deep-set under bushy brows conveyed a certain calm assurance, but Tom knew that time was of the essence. Even the most able soldier could do nothing about the weather and that was their worst enemy at present.

★ ★ ★

Back at his ranch Jack Hartigan watched as the additional men he had hired unloaded the crate they had brought with them. He called out to them to make sure that the precious cargo remained dry. One of his men asked what it was.

'It's that new stuff that's being made in Sweden, dynamite.'

'What does it do, Mr Hartigan?'

The rancher chuckled. 'It blasts everything to hell, like gunpowder, only much better. If we run into any trouble in town, that stuff will take care of it.'

'I thought we weren't expecting any trouble.'

Hartigan looked up at the ranch hand, a young man of about twenty. 'I'll give you a piece of advice, son. You should always expect trouble and that way you'll stay prepared. Tom Taylor left Paradise to get some help for Casey and I sent Abe Morgan after him. Abe hasn't arrived back yet, which could mean he never caught up with that half-breed, or did and came off worse.'

'So Casey could have some help comin' that we don't know about?' said the younger man nervously.

'That's right, but don't you worry about it. I think we can promise Casey's friends a big surprise.'

Ellen quietly closed her tiny bedroom window and climbed down from the chair, her mind racing. Even if Tom succeeded in finding help in time, those explosives provided Hartigan with a powerful weapon. She sat on the edge of her bed, thinking hard and then, slowly, a possible solution dawned on her.

The youth who had been standing outside with Hartigan was the one who had brought her lunch. She struck up a conversation with him, asking his name.

'I'm Calvin Peterson, but folks just call me Cal,' he told her.

'I was watching from the window when Mr Hartigan was telling you about the dynamite.'

Cal looked around nervously. 'I don't reckon I should be talkin' to you about that, Miss Garrett.'

Ellen smiled at him. 'I won't tell anyone if you don't. Besides, you seem like a nice young man and I wouldn't like to see you get hanged.'

The boy looked at her suspiciously. 'What do you mean? I ain't killed nobody.'

'No, but who do you think might be coming to help Mr Casey and stop your boss?'

Cal shrugged. 'How should I know? Mr Hartigan says that half-breed might have some Indian friends: Mexicans or maybe some outlaws.'

Ellen nodded. 'He might, but Fort Bowie is only two days' ride from here. The army are supposed to be in charge of the south-west, aren't they?'

'I guess so, but I ain't scared,' said the boy defiantly.

'What do you think happens to men who blow up soldiers? That's treason, isn't it?'

Cal looked scared and uncertain. 'Well, it's Mr Hartigan who's in charge, so I guess he's responsible for what happens.'

Ellen shook her head. 'If you're there and take part in what's going on you'll be committing treason too. Don't you think that the army will want to catch those responsible and punish them?'

The boy ran his hand through a tousled mop of fair hair. 'What can I do? I can't stop Mr Hartigan all by myself.'

'No, but you could go into town and warn Mr Casey. If the soldiers get here, he can at least tell them.'

Cal thought for a moment. 'All right, I'll do it. I ain't gonna hang for nobody, not even Mr Hartigan.' Then he put down the tray of food and was gone.

★　★　★

When Cal arrived at the jail Clem Bailey and Dr Maddox were with Jimmy. Haltingly, Cal told them about the dynamite and his conversation with Ellen. When he had finished the three men questioned him about where the explosives were being kept.

'There's a crate of the stuff in an outhouse, but it's guarded all the time.'

'Maybe we could sneak in there tonight and blow it up,' suggested Maddox.

Jimmy shook his head. 'I don't know much about dynamite. We could easily blow up the entire ranch and Ellen along with it.'

'We could just steal it,' suggested Clem.

'The crate's real heavy,' Cal said. 'You'd need a wagon.'

'A wagon would make too much noise and we'd be seen,' Jimmy told them. 'We'll just have to wait for the cavalry to get here. Anything else is too damned risky.' He turned to the boy. 'Let us know if you find out more.'

'I will, Mr Casey.' Then he stepped out of the jail and they watched sunshine stream in as he opened the door.

'At least the rain has stopped,' said Maddox. 'Let's hope that the ground dries out quickly. Hartigan's due here at noon the day after tomorrow and my guess is he'll come right on time.'

'With luck, the cavalry could be here tomorrow night,' said Jimmy.

'Yeah, with luck,' agreed Clem. 'Let's just hope ours hasn't run out.'

* * *

The troops riding towards Paradise were caked with mud and progress was slow as they trudged through the wet sand. Tom was starting to regain his strength but worry gnawed at his insides. Captain Marcus poked his head through the flap once more to ask how he was.

'I'm fine, but can't we move any faster?'

The officer shook his head. 'Not until the ground dries out, I'm afraid. I don't want to risk lame horses or an overturned wagon.'

'I'm just anxious about getting there in time.'

'I know and I can't guarantee that your friend will still be alive by the time we arrive. However, I can promise to restore law and order to Paradise and Jack Hartigan will get the punishment he deserves.'

Tom thanked him. Marcus was doing his best but his words were small comfort at the moment. He had hoped to be back by nightfall the next day, but that looked increasingly unlikely. An extra night would be spent camped out in the desert followed by an early start and a quick march to make it to Paradise for noon. Then, twenty exhausted soldiers would face Hartigan's men and try to rescue both Jimmy and Ellen, provided they were not too late.

The cavalry's progress continued to be slow throughout the day and by dusk, when they made camp, they were all exhausted. Fortunately, it remained dry overnight and they were able to move more quickly the next morning, despite the oppressive heat.

Back in Paradise, Hartigan continued to wait for Abe Morgan's return but his hopes were rapidly fading. He glanced at his pocket watch shortly after midday, realizing that if his most trusted employee was not back by nightfall, then some mishap must have befallen him.

'It must have been that damned half-breed or his Apache friends,' Hartigan muttered to himself as he lit a cigar. He made a mental note to ensure that Taylor was captured alive if possible, should he return to Paradise. It would be good to avenge Abe's death as well as his son's. Hartigan blew out a plume of smoke as he watched his men working in the hot sun. In twenty four hours he would bring Casey back to the ranch and hang him. The body would be left for the buzzards to eat for a few days, then taken down and burned. He smiled as he sat and smoked on his front porch. Hartigan was happy to wait, reflecting that revenge was indeed a dish that is best served when cold.

★ ★ ★

Another afternoon turned to dusk. The cavalry were still some distance from Paradise and Marcus refused Tom's request that they continue their journey into the night.

'Both men and horses are exhausted. I can't risk us arriving in a hostile situation without having had enough rest. From what you've told me about Hartigan, he's likely to put up one hell of a fight and we all need to be ready for him.'

Tom was forced to agree and spent another night in the wagon. The next morning he felt well enough to ride and was mounted on Banjo near the head of the column when they set off again at dawn. The hours went by quickly and his anxiety decreased as he slowly realized that they were going to make it in time. At last, at eleven o'clock, the town loomed out of the desert ahead of them. Tom rode on ahead and saw Jimmy standing with Clem and Dr Maddox in the street just outside the jail. He drew to a halt beside them and jumped down, wincing as he did so.

'Hey, you've been hurt,' said Jimmy, noticing the bandage on his friend's shoulder.

'Abe Morgan took a shot at me, but I got the bullet out myself and the doctor at the fort fixed me up.'

Jimmy watched as the cavalry rode in behind Tom. 'What happened to Morgan?'

Tom drew his finger across his throat. 'He won't be bothering us again. What's been happening around here?'

Jimmy's expression was grave. 'Hartigan's got a box of dynamite and he's prepared to use it.'

'That's going to make things damned difficult.' The words were spoken by

Captain Marcus and Tom quickly introduced the officer to Jimmy and his companions.

'Are you three men all the help we can expect against Hartigan and his gang?' asked the captain.

'I guess so,' replied Maddox. 'Most people here just want to be left in peace. They don't realize that there can never be any while they refuse to stand up to the likes of Hartigan.'

'Those are wise words. Right now I wish more people believed them,' replied Marcus.

'What do you figure on doin' about that dynamite?' asked Clem.

Marcus looked around him. 'I think the best thing to do is to spread my men around the town as much as possible. At least that way Hartigan can't blow us all up at once. We'll try to encircle him if we can. Do you know how many men he has?'

Jimmy shrugged. 'He lost quite a few in that last attack, when he tried to burn the place down. I think he can probably still rustle up as many men as you've got.'

'All right, here's what we're going to do,' said Marcus. He proceeded to outline his plan.

*   *   *

Meanwhile, Hartigan was instructing his men in the use of the dynamite before they set off for Paradise, holding up a stick to demonstrate. 'The nitroglycerine inside the paper wrapper causes the explosion when it's ignited after you light the fuse,' he explained. 'The stuff is packed with sawdust to make it more stable but you still have to be careful with it.' Each man was then handed a few sticks tied together with fuse wire. The remainder was stored in a crate in the back of a wagon. The canvas awning had been removed and replaced with a cage constructed from stakes of wood.

Hartigan was seated in his wheelchair but had hitched a horse to it so that he could drive it like a small carriage. He drove over to where the cage stood and looked at it admiringly. 'This will be Casey's prison. He'll be brought back to the ranch in it this afternoon and left inside until I decide it's time for his hanging. I'll fire anyone who gives him food or water. Is that clear?'

A murmur of assent ran through the assembled men and Ellen was then led out, bound, on horseback. Hartigan grinned at her. 'I'm so glad you could join us, Miss Garrett.'

'May God punish you for what you're about to do,' she told him.

'There's no God to punish or protect anybody. The sooner you realize that the better,' he replied. Then he gave the order to move out, unaware that Cal had already slipped away and was on his way to the jail.

* * *

The young ranch hand leaped from his sweating horse and hammered at the

182

door of the jail. 'Come on, open up. They're coming!'

'All right son, just hold on there a minute,' muttered Clem as he fumbled with the keys before admitting him.

Cal breathlessly described how Hartigan had distributed sticks of dynamite among his men, saying that the remainder was stored in the caged wagon that the rancher was bringing into town to collect his prisoner.

'Bringing that crate with him could turn out to be Hartigan's undoing,' said Jimmy.

'What do you mean?' asked Tom.

'I've got an idea. Now, you go with Cal and here's what I want you to do.'

Maddox smiled as Jimmy outlined his plan. 'It's very simple but it should work. I'll just go tell Captain Marcus so he knows what we intend to do.'

★　★　★

The streets of Paradise were deserted when Hartigan drove through town at the head of his gang, flanked by two riders armed with rifles. Jimmy stood in the road outside the jail, Clem and Dr Maddox beside him. Hartigan drew to a halt and noted with evident satisfaction that Maddox was holding a gun to Jimmy's head.

'You don't seem to have any friends left, Casey. What happened to that half-breed?'

Jimmy shrugged. 'Tom's not here.'

'I sent Abe Morgan after him when your friend left town. Abe hasn't come back yet. Do you know anything about that?'

Jimmy shook his head. 'How should I know?'

Hartigan stared hard at him. 'I might go a little easier on you if you tell me the truth.'

'Tom ran out on me. I guess he figured the situation was hopeless.'

Hartigan chuckled, satisfied now. 'Well, that's enough small talk for now. Move towards me very slowly. These boys here will be watching every step.'

Maddox answered him. 'Not so fast, Mr Hartigan. Release Miss Garrett first, and then we'll hand over Casey.'

Hartigan hesitated and Maddox continued. 'Look, nobody's offering you any resistance. You can see that we're about to hand him over but we don't trust you to let the girl go once you've got Casey.'

'I get it, you want to rest easy with your consciences, to be able say you did it to save an innocent girl's life and not just to protect your two-bit town,' sneered Hartigan.

'I guess you could put it like that,' said Maddox drily.

There was a tense silence, then Hartigan agreed. 'All right, we'll do things your way if it means less trouble. Bring Miss Garrett.'

Ellen's horse was led to the front, her hands were untied and she dismounted. One of the ranch hands shoved her forward and she ran over to Jimmy. Maddox stood aside while the couple embraced.

'That's enough!' shouted Hartigan. 'Casey, get your ass over here. My men have their rifles aimed at you and the girl.'

'Don't worry,' whispered Jimmy to Ellen as he gently removed her arms from around his neck. 'It's all part of the plan.'

At that moment Cal was lighting the oil soaked sagebrush and handing it to Tom. 'Do you think this will work?' he asked nervously.

'It'll have to or we're all in big trouble,' replied Tom. He crept out from their hiding place and darted halfway across the street. The box of dynamite burst into flames as soon as the sagebrush landed on top of it and Tom threw himself to the ground. Jimmy was still some distance from Hartigan when the explosion flung men and horses into the air. The windows in some nearby houses were shattered and the pungent smell of burning flesh hung in the air as thick clouds of smoke enveloped Hartigan and his surviving followers. When it cleared there was no sign of Jimmy or his companions, but from doorways, windows and rooftops scattered along the main street Captain Marcus and his men began firing.

There was no time to light fuses or throw the remaining sticks of dynamite as men were hit and fell to the ground. Hartigan screamed at his terrified followers to stand their ground and return fire, but by the time they were able to do so more than half of them had been killed. Seeing that they had become easy targets, he then ordered a retreat and they all backed off down the street, desperately looking for cover. Some of the men found shelter and fired back at their assailants, hitting several soldiers.

Hartigan drew to a halt around the side of a shattered storefront and a few of his men huddled around him. He asked if any of them had any dynamite left. One man held up a bundle of sticks.

'OK, let's wait a minute. Some of

them will come out and move further along the street now that they've got us on the run. When that happens, we'll throw the dynamite and then get the hell out while we still can.'

'What about Casey?' one of the men asked.

'Sooner or later, he'll come after us. Next time, we'll fight him on home ground.'

★   ★   ★

Further up the street Jimmy huddled in a doorway behind Captain Marcus. The officer raised a hand and waved at those behind to indicate that they should move forward, and they scurried cautiously down the road. Someone shot at them from a shop window and a trooper beside Jimmy hit the dust, a bullet hole between his eyes. Jimmy moved swiftly to return fire and one of Hartigan's men tumbled through the window, shattering the glass as his body fell to the ground.

Jimmy and his companions inched further forward, stepping among the burnt and bloodied remains of both men and horses. He sensed a movement from behind one of the buildings and turned as the bundle of dynamite, its fuse hissing, sailed towards them. He shouted a warning and fired at the missile so that it exploded in midair. The blast lifted him off his feet and he was flung back on to the ground, stunned. As the dust and smoke cleared, he came to and slowly managed to get up. Two men had been killed and the others had been knocked to the ground. Jimmy turned and helped Marcus to his feet.

'Look over there,' said the captain, pointing ahead.

In the distance, Jimmy saw Hartigan and some of his men making their way out of town. 'Damn, we can't just let them get away!'

'Take it easy, Mr Casey,' Marcus told him. 'We got Miss Garrett back and suffered relatively few casualties in the process while Hartigan and his men have taken a real beating.'

'But aren't you going to arrest him?'

'Of course, but let's bury our dead first. Hartigan's not going anywhere.'

Jimmy shrugged. 'I guess not; he still wants his revenge.'

Marcus dusted himself down. 'That's what I'm counting on. Let him brood on his ranch for a few hours. It'll give him a chance to get mad.'

'That will also give him time to get prepared.'

'No, it will give us time to get prepared. We need to know the layout of his ranch before we decide anything.'

Jimmy had a sudden thought. 'Come and meet Cal,' he said.

9

An hour later Jimmy was sitting around a table in the saloon with Captain Marcus, Tom, Clem, Dr Maddox, Cal and Ellen, studying the plan of the ranch which Cal had drawn for them.

'You said that the stables haven't been rebuilt yet. Does that mean that all the horses are kept in the corral overnight?' asked Marcus.

Cal nodded. 'Yes, that's right.'

The officer turned to Tom. 'Right, it will be your job to let those horses out so that no one can escape. Do you think you can manage that?'

'Sure, no problem,' he replied eagerly.

Marcus then marked the areas where ranch hands were normally posted on watch. 'Mr Casey, I suggest we take care of these men before entering the house to apprehend Hartigan. The rest of my troops will capture the men sleeping in the outhouse. Is that clear?'

'It all sounds very simple,' said Jimmy.

Marcus smiled. 'The best plans always are. Hartigan and his men will be demoralized and a swift attack at night should just about finish off any further resistance.'

'The maid and the housekeeper sleep here,' Ellen told them, pointing to a couple of rooms marked on the upper storey.

'Don't worry,' Marcus assured her. 'They won't come to any harm. Now, I suggest that we all try to get some rest before tonight.' He quickly rolled up the plan, then climbed upstairs to take a nap in one of the hotel rooms.

'The townsfolk are figurin' us all to be heroes for seein' off Hartigan today,' said Clem once Marcus had gone.

Jimmy sat back in his chair. 'I guess that just shows how fickle people can be. This morning they were happy to see me handed over for execution.'

Ellen laid a hand on his arm. 'Not everyone can be as brave as you. They did try to put up a fight at first.'

Jimmy drained the last of his whiskey. 'It's easy to fight when you think you're going to win. If Marcus asked for volunteers to go to the ranch tonight, they'd all be lining up at the door. No, the time to really fight is when it's because you've got right on your side, even if you're outnumbered and you've got your back against the wall.'

'Sometimes people need a brave man to show them that, to lead the way,' said Maddox thoughtfully.

'Yeah, I reckon if you stood for sheriff you'd win easy,' added Clem.

Jimmy shook his head. 'I've got other plans, I'm afraid.'

Ellen took his hand. 'We could change them. This could be a good place to settle down, with Hartigan gone.'

'You should at least think about it,' Tom said.

Jimmy frowned thoughtfully. 'This

place could do with some changes. Maybe I'm the man to do it, maybe not, but I'll think about it.'

* * *

Hartigan sat behind the desk in his study and called his remaining men in to see him. He opened a cashbox and he divided the contents into wads of cash. He handed one to each of them.

'What's goin' on, boss?' asked one of them in puzzlement.

'You men have all been loyal, stuck your necks out for me and done everything I've asked you to. Now it's over and time for you to go.'

'But them soldiers will be comin' here. What are you gonna do?' asked another of his men in alarm.

'You just let me worry about that. We can't fight the US army and win so I'm ordering you all to get out while you still can.'

'Do you figure on surrenderin', then?' asked the man who had spoken last.

Hartigan grimaced. 'Not exactly, but I've got one last job I want done before you leave. I need you to carry some things upstairs for me: they won't all fit in the elevator.' Then, once he was sitting in his wheelchair on the upper landing, Hartigan dismissed his house-keeper and the maid, gathered the items he required for his last stand and settled down quietly to wait.

★   ★   ★

It was midnight when a weary band of soldiers, accompanied by Jimmy, Tom and Clem, set off for Hartigan's ranch. Ellen and Dr Maddox saw them off.

'You don't have to do this, Jimmy,' urged Ellen. 'It's the army's job to take care of Hartigan now.'

'Miss Garrett's right,' added Marcus. 'You've risked more to defend this town than anyone. I won't think less of you for backing out now.'

Jimmy shook his head. 'No, this all started with me and I have to help finish it. I won't be able to live with myself if I walk away now.'

Ellen nodded slowly. 'I understand. Just try to come back safely.'

Jimmy smiled. 'Don't worry. If I was still a gambling man I'd give myself pretty good odds.'

They slowed their horses to a trot and spread out slowly as they reached their destination. The ranch was eerily silent and neither Jimmy nor Marcus could find anyone on guard. Behind them, a branch snapped and they both turned round.

'It's me,' hissed Tom. 'All the horses are gone.'

Then Clem's voice whispered that there was no one in the outhouse either. 'They must all have gone to Mexico or someplace; been scared off, I reckon.'

'No, that's not it,' said Jimmy. 'Hartigan won't quit until one of us is dead, so he must have something else in mind.'

Suddenly, lights appeared from the upper windows of the house and a voice called down to them. 'I know you're there, Casey. I've been expecting you.'

'We've got the place surrounded,' shouted Marcus. 'Are you willing to surrender?'

Hartigan laughed in response. 'There's just one way to settle this. I've got a gun and so has Casey. All my men have gone now, so let him come in to face me alone!'

Jimmy moved towards the door and Marcus seized his arm. 'It could be a trick. I'll send my men in.'

'No, this is between me and him now. If I need help, I'll call you.'

'All right but if you're not out in five minutes we're coming in. Is that clear?'

Jimmy nodded his agreement and stepped on to the porch. He moved into the hall which was dimly lit from the oil lamps burning on the upper storey. There was a strong smell of whiskey and the floor felt sticky under his feet. Hartigan sat in his bath chair at the top of the stairs and gave a grim smile of satisfaction as he watched Jimmy approach.

'Come on up here, Casey, and let's get this settled.'

Jimmy slowly began to climb the staircase but paused when he got halfway.

'Don't worry, I won't draw on you until you're up here,' Hartigan assured him, then he reversed his chair back along the upper landing.

Jimmy continued climbing the stairs; he had almost reached the top when his adversary threw an oil lamp over the banister. It smashed on the whiskey-sodden floor below where the combination of oil, alcohol, wooden furniture and curtains caused tongues of flame to shoot up immediately.

'You crazy bastard!' shouted Jimmy as he leaped back in alarm. He felt the searing heat immediately and saw with dismay that his escape route from the house was now blocked by the rapidly spreading fire.

There was whiskey on the floor of the upper landing, too, and Jimmy noticed that there were several empty bottles scattered about. Hartigan held up another oil lamp as his cackles of laughter echoed throughout the empty house.

'Are you ready to draw yet, Casey? If you shoot, I'll drop this lamp and *whoosh!*'

Jimmy shook his head in astonishment. 'You're crazy,' was all he could say.

'No, I'm not. I just figured I wasn't gonna come out of this mess alive anyway so I might as well take you with me.'

Jimmy was now standing by a door, he recalled from Cal's plan of the ranch that it led to the main guest room which had a veranda. Realizing that it was his only chance of escape he began turning the handle, but the door was locked.

Hartigan laughed again. 'So long, Casey!' he cried as he hurled the lamp across the landing. Jimmy fired at the lock and burst through the door as the flames surrounded him. He staggered through the smoke and burning heat to jump through the window. The glass shattered around him and flames scorched his back as he vaulted over the veranda and then dropped through the air to the ground below. The last thing he heard before being knocked out by the fall was Hartigan's howl of despair upon seeing his enemy escape. Then the fire finally consumed the embittered rancher.

*   *   *

When Jimmy awoke, he learned that he had suffered few injuries apart from a large bump on the back of his head, some bruises, minor burns and a pair of singed eyebrows. With some reluctance he agreed to spend a day in bed while Ellen fussed over him. Once he was up and about, however, he immediately set about packing his things for his onward journey to Tucson. Then he went with Ellen to the livery stables to collect Banjo and bid Clem farewell.

'Tom's gonna stick around, so I figure on makin' him a partner in the business. I've no family to speak of and I'd be happy to leave it all to him in time,' Clem told them.

'It's good to hear that all this killing has not been entirely in vain,' said Ellen.

Clem puffed thoughtfully on his pipe. 'Yeah, that ain't all. Folks want to make Paradise live up to its name now that old Hartigan's gone. Maybe you should stop by the town square on your way out and hear what's goin' on.'

They did so and found Captain Marcus reading a declaration to a crowd of assembled citizens. 'By the power invested in me as a representative of the military government of the south west, I hereby give notice that the property of the late Frank Hartigan has been confiscated due to his illegal activities, and handed over to the town of Paradise. In consultation with the town council, it has been agreed that Jimmy Casey should be offered the position of sheriff in recognition of his efforts to protect Paradise and its citizens from the depredations of Frank Hartigan and his gang.' The officer paused and looked directly at Jimmy. 'Well, Mr Casey, what do you say?'

The crowd parted and Jimmy made his way to the front. Marcus handed him a star-shaped badge made of tin and he studied it for a moment. Then he addressed the crowd.

'I had to fight Hartigan; he gave me no other choice, but when he threatened this town one man selflessly risked his life to bring the cavalry here. That same man destroyed the gang's explosives even though he could have ridden away from this situation at any time. Now, I've heard it said that a half-breed can't be the sheriff of Paradise, but if you really want to change your town I think that you should give the job to the man who had less reason than any of us to help you. I propose Tom Taylor as the new sheriff of Paradise!'

A murmur ran through the crowd;

there were whispered discussions, then one man called out: 'Yeah, let's have Tom Taylor for sheriff!' Soon he was joined by others until the entire crowd was shouting Tom's name. Then Captain Marcus raised his hands and the people fell silent. He called Tom forward and, with a look of amazement, the half-breed made his way to the front. A cheer went up as Jimmy pinned the badge to Tom's shirtfront.

'Good luck. Between this and Clem's horses, you'll have your work cut out,' said Jimmy as the two men shook hands.

'Thanks, Jimmy. I never expected this.'

'You've earned it. Like I said, you helped out here when you could have just walked away and that took guts.'

* * *

'Do you think you made the right decision?' asked Ellen later as they rode away from Paradise.

'I think so,' replied Tom. 'The town needs to move on from what happened and I would always have been a reminder of the past. They wanted to make me sheriff because they felt guilty for not standing up to Hartigan; that's hardly the best way to make a new start.'

'Is that what we're doing, making a new start?'

'I guess we are.'

'Does that mean no more card tricks?'

'Hey, I never used tricks but no, I won't be playing cards any more.'

Ellen gave him a smile of satisfaction. 'I'm glad to hear it. Let's hope that's an end to all our troubles.'

They rode further on across the Arizona Basin, but this time Jimmy surveyed the arid landscape with a feeling of contentment. There was no one after him, he was in the company of the woman he loved and every mile they rode brought them closer to the new start they had spoken of. Reaching higher ground, they passed through a narrow canyon which Jimmy recalled from his previous journey when he had been on his way to Paradise. Suddenly he froze and raised a hand to indicate that Ellen should stop behind him. That sixth sense of his, which had served him well so often in the past, told him that they were being watched.

'Stop right there, Casey. You're surrounded.' The voice came from above and he looked up to see men armed with rifles standing in two groups of three atop each ridge of the canyon. Then another dishevelled figure stepped out in front of him, holding a rifle.

It took Jimmy a few moments to recognize the scarred and burned face before him and realize the horrific truth. 'I thought you were dead,' he began.

'So did them Apaches. They left me for dead when they'd done their worst, but I sure fooled 'em all.' He raised his hat and Ellen turned away at the sight of where his scalp had once been.

'I didn't even cry out,' he told them triumphantly. 'Hate kept me alive, that and the waterhole I managed to crawl to. Then I ran into these boys when Jack Hartigan paid 'em off, and they looked after me real good.'

'It's over, Morgan. Hartigan's dead, the army will be after you and these men of yours. Why don't you just let it go?'

'You're wastin' time, Casey. Throw down that gunbelt and get off your horse. Do it slow or I'll put a bullet in you and one in her for good measure.'

Jimmy reluctantly began to obey. 'Use your left hand,' Abe prompted him. The other members of the gang now started to climb down and gathered around. Two of them bound Ellen's hands to her horse's saddle and her feet to the stirrups while another kept her covered with a pistol.

'Bein' gentlemen an' all, we'll let Miss Garrett ride, but you'd best get down from that horse like I told you,' said Abe, gesturing with his rifle.

Jimmy dismounted slowly and the two men faced each other. Abe's eyes were narrow slits in his shattered face, but they seemed to burn with hatred.

'Where's that half-breed friend of yours?' he demanded.

Jimmy shrugged noncommittally and Abe jammed a rifle barrel into his stomach. Jimmy fell to his knees as pain ripped through him. The former ramrod stood over him.

'You're no good without them fancy pistols of yours, Casey. I asked you a question, now gimme an answer.'

'You can go to hell,' said Jimmy.

Abe raised the rifle once more but Ellen screamed at him to stop. He paused and looked up at her.

'Tom's the new sheriff of Paradise,' she told him.

Abe laughed, showing a row of broken teeth, and his men joined in. 'Is that a fact? Well, a half-breed sheriff. I never thought I'd see the day. We might just have to call in and see old Tom.

Maybe we'll find out how quick on the draw he is.'

Jimmy staggered to his feet. 'The army's there now. Why don't you just let it go?'

Abe shrugged. 'Them soldier boys will be movin' on in a day or two. I'd say our business with Tom can wait until then. In the meantime, we got plans for you.'

The men all got back on their horses, Abe pausing to retrieve Jimmy's gun-belt. 'I reckon this'll make a fine souvenir of our acquaintance,' he remarked, chuckling.

The gang now gathered around him, their mount's hoofs throwing up dust as they circled threateningly. Jimmy looked up searchingly at their faces and swallowed hard to contain his fear. What were they going to do next?

A moment later a rope sang through the air and he found himself caught like a steer, the cord bound tightly around him, pinning his arms to his chest. Abe whooped with delight and the men set off at a brisk pace, pulling their prisoner behind. Jimmy was forced to run in order to keep up as the gang members made their way further into the desert. He stumbled over rocks a couple of times and found himself dragged along the baking sand until he managed to get to his feet again.

After an hour of this, Jimmy cut a sorry figure. His clothes were now torn and caked with dust from the times he had fallen, his body was battered and bruised. He had lost his hat and his face was starting to blister in the heat. When he fell once more, he could barely summon the strength to rise.

At this point, Ellen intervened. 'For God's sake, stop it,' she pleaded with Abe. 'Whatever you think he's done, Jimmy never treated anyone this way.'

Abe held up his hand and called them to a halt. 'The lady's right,' he said, taking a swig from his canteen. 'We've had our fun; let's just get on with it.'

'What are you going to do?' she asked nervously.

'We're gonna hang him. The boys told me that was Jack Hartigan's plan before the army interfered.'

'You heard what Jimmy said earlier. Hartigan's dead. Let his hate die with him.'

'Hate don't die so easy,' responded Abe with a cackle.

One of the men pointed to a tree standing on a plateau up ahead. 'I reckon that'll take Casey's weight,' he suggested.

Abe shrugged. 'It's as good a place as any. If you know any prayers, Miss Garrett, I suggest you start sayin' 'em pronto.'

'Please, just let me go to him for a few minutes to give him a last drink of water and say goodbye.'

Abe looked hard at her while he considered this, then his gaze softened slightly. 'I guess it don't make no difference and I got nothin' against you, anyhow.' He leaned over and cut her bonds before handing her the canteen. 'Make it quick,' he added.

Ellen dismounted and hurried over to where Jimmy was now sitting up, slumped against a rock. She handed him the canteen and he drank from it greedily. Then she soaked a bandanna and wiped it over his face and neck.

'They mean to hang you,' she whispered urgently.

'I figured it would be something like that. Do you think you could play for time, give me a chance to rest up a little? I've got a plan but I just need to get some of my strength back.'

Ellen nodded and walked back to where Abe sat on his horse, waiting impatiently. 'Jimmy's completely exhausted, but he has a last request.'

'What is it?'

'He wants to walk to his death, not be dragged like an animal. Could you let him rest for a little while?'

'He'll have all the rest he needs soon enough,' said Abe with a broken-toothed grin.

'The horses are tired and I reckon we could do with stoppin' ourselves,' said one of the gang members. The man who had spoken stuffed some tobacco into the bowl of his pipe. 'Besides, it can't hurt to give Casey time to dwell on it and get real scared.'

'Yeah, you're right,' conceded Abe. He turned back to Ellen. 'You can go on back there and sit with him if you like,' he added roughly.

A half-hour passed while they all rested. Jimmy drank more water from the canteen and gradually a little strength returned to his aching limbs. He just hoped that it would be enough for what he planned to do. Then Abe walked over to them, holding a rifle.

'Your time is up, Casey. Come on, get to your feet. You too, Miss Garrett.'

They got up slowly and Abe gestured for them to walk ahead of him towards the tree, which now had a rope slung around one of its branches, ending in a noose. The gang member with the pipe brought Jimmy's horse alongside him.

'It's like I explained to your sweet-heart. Jack Hartigan meant for you to hang, so I figured out how to make the necessary arrangements,' Abe told him. 'It'd be a shame to let old Jack down now, wouldn't it?'

'Do what you want with me but let Ellen go,' pleaded Jimmy.

'That's very noble of you, Casey,' replied Abe mockingly. 'I'll just leave you to wonder about what we're gonna do with her while you're on the end of that rope.'

'You're a coward, Morgan. You just don't have the guts to face me in a fight.'

Abe shrugged. 'It don't make no difference to me what you think. I'm gonna hang you and that's the end of it. I don't see no reason to give you a chance to get away.'

'Look at the state of me. I'm in no position to get away. Give me a gun with one bullet in the chamber and then we'll draw. If I kill you the girl goes free but your men can still hang me.'

Abe shook his head. 'I know you're

faster than me. Why should I give you a deal like that?'

'What if I put my hands behind my head? That would slow me down a lot and you haven't exactly left me in good condition after that journey back there.'

A murmur ran through the other members of the gang and they began urging their leader to accept Jimmy's offer. Abe looked around nervously. He was still not sure he could beat Jimmy, but he did not want to appear scared in front of his men.

'Give him back his gunbelt with one gun in it and one bullet in the chamber,' he ordered as his men whooped with delight.

Jimmy buckled on his weapon and noted that his other pistol had been discarded, lying several yards away on the ground. It was just as he had hoped. He placed his hands behind his head as agreed while Abe threw down his rifle and prepared to draw. As the former ramrod went for his gun, Jimmy's hands came down in a lightning-quick movement and he spun sideways, firing as Abe's bullet whizzed past him. Jimmy's shot went straight through his adversary's heart and Abe crumpled to the ground. Before the other gang members had time to recover from their surprise, Jimmy had dived to the ground, retrieved the other nickel-plated Colt .45, which he fired in an arc along the line of men.

Five men fell dead, only two of whom managed to fire their guns, but where was the sixth? Suddenly there was a scream from behind and he turned to see that the last gang member was pointing a gun at him while his left arm was locked around Ellen's throat.

'Throw that gun as far as you can, Casey, or the girl dies,' said the last gang member.

Jimmy shook his head. 'No, you'll shoot us both.'

The gang member grinned. 'That's a chance you'll have to take, but I've got six bullets and you've only got one, so you'd better do as I say.'

'You're forgetting one thing,' Jimmy told him.

'What's that?'

'I'm a better shot than you.' A bullet hit the gang member between the eyes before Jimmy had finished the sentence and Ellen ran to him, sobbing with relief as she collapsed into his arms.

'It's all over now; there's nothing to be afraid of,' he told her soothingly. 'Hartigan, Abe and his men are all dead now. There's no one left to come after us.'

'Are you sure?' she asked, raising a tear stained face to look at him.

'I promise you that it will be just storekeeping from now on. No more guns, no more cards and no more desperate men trying to hang me or gun me down.'

Then Ellen smiled at last and reached up to kiss him. 'If we hadn't just left there I'd say that sounds like Paradise.'

'Oh, there's more than one way to Paradise,' Jimmy told her as he returned her kiss.